Victoria Torres

Unfortunately Average

Victoria Torres, Unfortunately Average
is published by Stone Arch Books,
A Capstone Imprint
1710 Roe Crest Drive
North Mankato, Minnesota 56003
www.capstoneyoungreaders.com

Library of Congress Cataloging-in-Publication Data
Bowe, Julie, 1962– author.
  Face the music / by Julie Bowe.
      pages cm. —— (Victoria Torres, unfortunately average)
  Summary: Victoria Torres is the fifth chair out of nine flutes in her middle school band,
so when the director asks for a someone to play the new piccolo, Victoria sees it as her
chance to stand out——but her best friend Bea has also volunteered, and their friendship
may not survive the competition when they audition for the part.
  ISBN 978-1-4965-0534-7 (library binding)
  ISBN 978-1-4965-0538-5 (paperback)
  ISBN 978-1-4965-2359-4 (eBook pdf)
  ISBN 978-1-4965-2480-5 (reflowable ePub)
1. Bands (Music)——Juvenile fiction. 2. Musical instruments——Juvenile fiction. 3. Best
friends——Juvenile fiction. 4. Competition (Psychology)——Juvenile fiction. 5. Middle
schools——Juvenile fiction. 6. Hispanic American children——Juvenile fiction. 7. Middle-born
children——Juvenile fiction. [1. Bands (Music)——Fiction. 2. Musical instuments——Fiction. 3.
Best friends——Fiction. 4. Friendship——Fiction. 5. Competition (Psychology)——Fiction. 6.
Middle schools——Fiction. 7. Schools——Fiction. 8. Hispanic Americans——Fiction. 9. Middle-
born children——Fiction.] I. Title.
  PZ7.B671943Fac 2016
  813.6——dc23
  [Fic]   2015008951

Designer: Veronica Scott
Image credits: Capstone Studio
Design elements: Shutterstock

Special thanks to the team of tweens who provided helpful feedback
on covers and design.

Printed in the United States of America in Stevens Point, Wisconsin.
032015   008824WZF15

FACE THE MUSIC

by Julie Bowe

STONE ARCH BOOKS

a capstone imprint

All About Me

Hi, I'm Victoria Torres — Vicka for short. Not that I am short. Or tall. I'm right in the middle, otherwise known as "average height for my age." I'm almost twelve years old and just started sixth grade at Middleton Middle School. My older sister, Sofia, is an eighth grader. My little brother, Lucas, is in kindergarten, so that puts me in the middle of my family too:

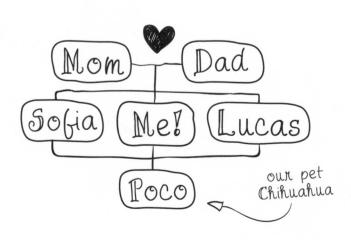

our pet Chihuahua

I'm average in other ways too. I live in a middle-sized house at the center of an average town. I get Bs for grades, sit in the middle of the flute section in band, and can hit a baseball only as far as the shortstop. And even though she would say I'm "above average," I'm not always the BEST best friend to my BFF, Bea.

Still, my parents did name me Victoria — as in victory? They had high hopes for me right from the start! This year, I am determined to be better than average in every way!

 Me!

Chapter 1

Xs and Os

"Stop sticking Nature Nibbles up your nose, Lucas," I say to my little brother on Saturday morning. "*Ewww! Don't eat them now!* Help me find the cordless phone so I can call Bea."

Lucas ignores me as I hunt between the couch cushions in our living room. He's watching cartoons and munching on dry cereal that looks like a bowl of gravel. Our mom thinks sugary cereal is bad for us, so she buys only the kind made from oats, bran, and tree bark, I think.

I have my own phone, but it's all the way upstairs,

and I'm in a hurry to call my BFF. Almost every weekend we hang out together, listening to music, playing video games, doing art projects, and baking gooey chocolate chip cookies. We are excellent cookie bakers. Best friends usually are!

"Move, Vicka!" Lucas shouts as I poke around him. "You're blocking the TV, and this is my favorite show!"

I glance at the television. "Is this the one about that talking toilet plunger?"

Lucas nods excitedly. "Toilet Plunger Paul! Today, he and his sidekick, Eraser Girl, are saving Dimpletown from an invasion of mutant dust bunnies! Do you want to watch with me?"

"I'd *love* to," I say in a voice that makes me sound as snarky as my sorta friend, Annelise. "But it's Saturday, otherwise known as *Bea*day. Have you seen the phone? Bea is probably wondering why I haven't called yet."

Lucas points toward the downstairs bathroom. "It's in Dad's executive office," he says.

"Thanks!" I reply, snagging a Nature Nibble from his bowl and popping it into my mouth as I dash to the bathroom. Dad calls it his *executive office* even though his real office is at the music store he and my uncle, Julio, own.

There, sitting on the sink next to a tube of Sophia's pimple medicine, is the phone. Sophia is fourteen. She keeps a phone and pimple medicine in every room of the house. Personally, I don't think the zit stick is doing her much good.

Punching the speed dial, I check myself out in the mirror while waiting for Bea to answer.

Score! No pimples.

Turning sideways, I can see that my hair is really getting long, but that's the only part of me that seems to be growing. In every other way, I am still completely average.

"Hello?"

At last! Bea!

"Hi! It's me. What took you so long to answer?"

9

"I had a hair emergency. I was out of scrunchy gel, so I had to beg some off of Jazmin. She made me pay her a dollar for two squirts! Stop laughing, Vicka — you know how annoying big sisters can be. Where are you? Inside a tunnel? Your voice sounds echoey."

"I'm in the bathroom," I explain.

"The *bathroom*? TMI, Vicka. Call me when you're done!"

"I'm not *doing* anything," I explain. "I'm just standing here, looking in the mirror."

"Oh," Bea replies. "Any new developments?"

I turn sideways again and study my slender frame. "Nope," I report. "You?"

"Nothing." Bea says with a sigh.

I smile, happy my BFF and I are still evenly matched when it comes to height, weight, and shoe size.

I wander into the hallway with the phone. "What do you want to do today?" I ask Bea. "Hang out here? Go to the library? Bake cookies?"

"Can't, can't, and . . . can't," Bea replies. "Remember? I have my winter recital today."

Bea takes private piano lessons. She also plays flute with me in our school band. Bea is a super-talented musician. She can even play "Jingle Bells" on her phone keypad!

"*¡Uf!*" I say. "I forgot about your recital. I'd come, but I promised Mom I'd watch Lucas this afternoon. She's scrapbooking here with her friends. What am I going to do without you?"

"Call Jenny?" Bea suggests. Jenny is my second best friend. She moved to Middleton last summer.

"Good idea," I say to Bea. "Maybe Jenny likes to bake cookies too."

"Save some for me!" Bea says before hanging up.

I call Jenny. "Sorry, Victoria," her dad says when I ask to speak with her. "Jen has a gymnastics meet this weekend. She and her mom won't get back until tomorrow."

¡Ay! Jenny is a super-fantastic gymnast, so I'm

happy she's cartwheeling and balancing and flying around. But I'm bummed she can't come over today.

I carry the phone into the living room and slump on the couch next to Lucas. Poco jumps onto my lap, wagging his tail and giving me doggie kisses. "Not now, Poco!" I say, laughing and pushing him down. "I'm trying to plan my day."

Poco settles onto my lap. I pet his silky fur while I try to think of other friends I could call. The list is short because I am only averagely popular.

I could call Katie or Grace, but they're just "school friends." We eat lunch together in the Caf and chat online sometimes, but I don't actually have their phone numbers.

Then there's Annelise. She's not one of my best friends, but I *do* have her phone number. I glance at Lucas. He's still sticking Nature Nibbles in his nose, then fake sneezing to see how far they fly.

"Look, Vicka!" Lucas shouts after an especially hard sneeze. "That one made it halfway to the TV!"

Poco hops off my lap, runs to the cereal nugget that Lucas just snot-shot, and eats it.

I make a disgusted face and ask myself a very important question: *Do I, Victoria Torres, want to spend the best day of the week with a cereal sneezer?*

Answer: *No, I do not.*

I call Annelise.

"Hello, Vicka," she says on the first ring. "I know it's you because I have caller ID on my brand-new phone. Daddy bought it for me yesterday. What do you want? I'm polishing my nails, so make it quick."

Annelise is one of the bossiest girls I know. She used to be one of the meanest too, but then she matured. "Do you want to come over? We could bake cookies."

I wait while she blows on her nails. "Why would I want to do that?" she finally asks. "They sell cookies at the European bakery downtown. That's where my mother buys all of our baked goods."

I roll my eyes even though Annelise can't see me.

"But it's fun to bake them yourself. Bea and I do it almost every weekend."

"Then why are you calling me?" Annelise asks. "Are you guys fighting or something?" Annelise sounds like she's hoping my answer will be yes. She loves to stir up drama between friends.

"No, Bea and I never fight," I reply. "She's just busy today."

"So I'm your second choice, huh?" Annelise says.

"Actually, you're my *third* choice, but don't take that the wrong way. Jenny is my second-best friend. You know that. But she's busy too."

Annelise does a smirky sniff. "Don't take *this* the wrong way, Vicka, but I have more important things to do than bake cookies with you. As soon as my nails dry, I'm going to the mall. My mother is buying my holiday dresses today."

"Dresses?" I say. "How many do you need?"

"Three," Annelise replies matter-of-factly. "One for the party at my dad's house. One for the party at my mom's house. And one for the holiday concert at school."

"Why can't you wear the same dress three times?" I ask.

Annelise sniffs again. "Because that would be totally boring. Besides, my mother is paying for them. I might as well get as many as I want."

I sigh. "Whatevs, Annelise. Gotta go."

"Have fun doing nothing with nobody," she quips. Then she laughs to herself before hanging up. I take back what I said earlier about her not being mean anymore.

I ditch the phone and go looking for Mom. Maybe she has time to take me shopping for my holiday dress too, before her scrapbooking party. Our school concert is only a few weeks away. Going to the mall would make this unfortunately average day feel a little more special.

But Mom is already setting out all her holiday scrapbooking stuff on the dining room table. She and her friends must be getting an early start on making holiday cards. No way will she have time to take me shopping.

Dad bops downstairs. "Don't wait up," he tells Mom, pecking her on the cheek. "I'll be home late."

Mom kisses him back. "Say hi to Julio for me."

"Where are you going?" I ask Dad. "Can Lucas and I come too?" My sister, Sofia, is at a math club meeting, but she probably wouldn't want to hang out with us anyway. All she wants to do on weekends is study for school or stare into her boyfriend's eyes.

"Working at the store, then driving into the city," he tells me. "Uncle Julio and I have a gig tonight!"

Dad and Uncle Julio are in a band called The Jalapeños. Uncle Julio sings and plays guitar. Dad sings too and plays the drums. I can't sing, and the only instrument I know how to play is the flute, but I'm a pretty good dancer! Dad grabs me and twirls me around the room singing one of the jazzy songs his band plays.

Mom applauds at the end of our dance. "Encore!" she says as Dad and I take a bow. I get ready to do another dance.

Dad kisses me on the top of my head. "No time for an encore now, Bonita." That's the nickname Dad gave to me when I was a baby. It means *pretty little one* in Spanish. "And I can't take you and Lucas along this time. See you tomorrow morning. What shall I make for breakfast. Pancakes?"

"*¡Sí!*" I say, hugging him goodbye. "With chocolate chips, *por favor.*"

Dad smiles. "Chocolate chip pancakes it is."

Fortunately, Dad doesn't mind a little sugar for breakfast!

After Dad leaves, I sit at the table and fiddle with a pair of Mom's fancy scissors, feeling sorry for myself. I don't have a favorite cartoon to watch or a club meeting to attend or a job or even a hobby! I'm not a great gymnast or musician. And I don't have tons of money to spend at the mall.

I'm just me, Victoria Torres, unfortunately average from the inside out.

"Everyone has something special to do today, except me," I grump.

Mom looks up from sorting through a bunch of stickers. "You could make cards with us," she offers.

I sigh. I like making crafty things with Bea, but it doesn't seem as much fun with Mom and her friends. They just sit around, drinking coffee and talking about grown-up stuff like the price of gasoline and where to find the best deal on pork chops and who has the most kids on the honor roll this year. As Annelise would say, *Boring*.

"Can I have some paper?" I ask, sifting through the stack of holiday designs Mom just set on the table. "Maybe I'll make some cards in my room."

"Sure!" Mom says. "Take what you want."

I grab a few sheets and head upstairs. Tossing the paper onto my desk, I crouch by my bed and reach under the mattress, pulling out the candy wrapper I keep hidden there. My crush, Drew, gave me a candy bar once. Technically, I bought it. But he handed it to me, so Bea says that counts as a gift from a boy. I was planning to keep the candy bar forever until Lucas ate it. *Grrr!*

At least he didn't eat the wrapper. I close my eyes, pressing it to my nose. It still smells like milk chocolate. That's the sweetest kind of candy bar there is. Drew told me so. I felt very special that day!

Maybe I should make a card for Drew? I've never given him anything before. He doesn't even know that I like him! The only person who knows that secret is Bea.

I walk over to my desk and fold a sheet of holiday paper into a card. Then I write a message inside it.

To: Drew
From: Your Secret Admirer

I smile as I read the words. It's easy to feel brave about crushing on a boy when it's a secret!

I draw some *Xs* and *Os* for *kisses* and *hugs*. It's also easy to feel brave about *kissing* a boy when it's only in writing.

I tuck the card under my mattress, along with the candy wrapper.

Then I slump against my bed, wishing Bea were here. Secrets feel more sparkly when you can share them with your best friend!

Chapter 2

A Big Surprise

It's chilly as I head out the door to school on Monday morning. This is the first day it's cold enough to wear my winter jacket, which makes me look like a big purple marshmallow. Not in a bad way though. I like marshmallows!

Stopping at the corner, I look down the street to watch for Bea. A moment later, I see her, waving to me. She looks like a marshmallow too, but she's a pink one!

"How was your recital?" I ask as Bea clomps up to me in boots that perfectly match her puffy jacket.

"It was great!" Bea replies. "I even got a standing ovation!"

"That's epic!" I link arms with Bea as we make our way to school. "My dad says every musician dreams of getting a standing O."

Bea nods. "Now we can focus on getting one at our holiday concert. Can you believe it? This will be our first big performance of middle school!" We've been practicing our band numbers for a few weeks, so the concert has really been on our minds lately.

Bea's eyes go glittery. "I can't wait to play in front of a packed auditorium! The choir will sing too, and there will be ensembles . . . maybe even soloists! The Booster Club always decks out the auditorium with tons of lights and decorations. I'm going to help decorate, are you?"

"Of course!" I say, catching Bea's excitement. "My parents are on the Booster Club, so we help every year. Sofia has been in the choir since she was in sixth grade."

"Jazmin sang a duet for the concert last year," Bea adds. "She and her friend wore matching red dresses and cute elf hats!"

"I remember that!" I say. "Maybe you and I could play a flute duet this year?"

"Great idea!" Bea says.

"Let's ask Mr. Ono right away." Mr. Ono is the middle school band director. "Last week he said there would be time for only a few ensembles."

Bea squares her shoulders. "Well, I am first chair of the flute section," she says, importantly. "If I want to play a duet, I'm sure Mr. Ono will let me. *Us*, I mean."

Bea is the first sixth grade student to ever sit in the first chair of our flute section. I don't even come close to being the best flute player. I sit in the *fifth* chair — exactly halfway between the first chair and the last chair. That's where Jenny sits. She's good, like me, but we don't shine, like Bea. Still, we have fun in band, along with our other friends. Katie plays French horn. Grace and Annelise play clarinet. They sit right behind me in band, which means I have to listen to a lot of whispering and squeaking. Grace is a chatterbox. And when Annelise plays the clarinet, it sounds like she's rubbing two balloons together.

We hurry down the last stretch of sidewalk to our school. It snowed last night, so it's covered with a soft layer of white flakes, like feathers after a slumber party pillow fight! I glance back as we walk along, smiling at the trail of footprints following us. After a long weekend with no Bea, I'm happy to be side by side with my bestie again.

When we get to our locker a few minutes later, Katie and Grace are there, admiring the new outfit Annelise is wearing. "I got new shoes too," she tells us. "They go with the dresses I bought. Wait until you see the one I'm wearing for the concert! It's green and covered with glitter! When the stage lights hit me, I'm going to totally shine. You guys better bring shades!"

"Should we bring ornaments too?" Jenny asks, looking over from her locker. "Then we could decorate you." Jenny can never resist taking swipes at Annelise when she's bragging. *Un*fortunately for Jenny, it usually comes back to bite her.

Annelise steams as Jenny gets Katie and Grace to join her in singing, "O Annelise tree, O Annelise tree, how lovely are your branches . . ." Bea and I join in too. It's a total giggle fest.

"Joke all you want," Annelise cuts in. "It doesn't bother me." Then she narrows her eyes at Jenny. "I'd rather have *glitter* on my dress than *tinsel* on my teeth!"

Jenny stops giggling and puts a hand over her mouth. She just got braces last week.

The bell rings and everyone takes off for class. Bea and I wait up for Jenny as she grabs stuff from her locker. "How was your gymnastics meet this weekend?" I ask as we walk down the hall together.

"It was fab!" Jenny replies. "I placed third in the

all-around competition!" She doesn't try to hide her smile now. She beams with pride, braces and all.

"Congrats!" I give Jenny a high five.

"Third place is good," Bea says. "But weren't you bummed that you didn't come in first?"

Jenny shrugs. "I was competing against girls from much bigger schools. They were übergood! I was happy just to get a medal."

Bea nods and smiles politely.

I give Jenny another high five as she ducks into her first hour class.

"I thought Jenny really cared about gymnastics," Bea says to me as we keep heading down the hallway together.

I push up my glasses and crinkle my eyebrows. "What do you mean? Jenny is crazy about gymnastics!"

Bea stops by our classroom. "If I got third place in a piano competition, I'd be a total wreck," she explains. "I'm not putting down Jenny, but when I compete for something that's important to me, I play to win."

Bea heads into class. I follow along, thinking about what she said. I play to win too, but most of the time I end up in the middle no matter how hard I try.

When it's time for band, I grab my flute and folder, take my seat, and pull out our concert music, setting all three songs on my stand. First up is "Still, Still, Still." Next is "Mistletoe Medley." And our grand finale number is "Sleigh Ride."

Other kids arrive, including Bea. Henry walks by. He sets down his tuba and snatches "Mistletoe Medley" from my stand, holding it over his head. A picture of bright green leaves with little white berries decorates the cover of the music. "Line up, ladies!" Henry shouts. "I'm standing under the *mistletoe*!" Then he walks around the band room, making smooching sounds at all the girls.

Henry is the biggest clown in our class. No one wants to kiss a clown! When he comes back around to Bea and me, Bea won't even look at him. I make a throw-up face.

"Aw, c'mon." Henry whimpers like Poco does when I don't have time to play fetch with him. "Someone must want to kiss me!" He looks at Bea. She looks away.

"Don't hold your breath, Hen," Drew says, coming up behind his best buddy and patting his shoulder. "Then again, maybe you *should* hold your breath. It might help. You *did* eat four slices of garlic cheese bread for lunch!"

Henry grins. "Five slices." Then he burps.

Drew waves his hand in front of his nose. He takes my mistletoe music from Henry and holds it over his head. "I only ate *three* slices. Let me give it a shot!"

Even though Drew is my crush, there is no way I would ever dare to kiss him, even if mistletoe was involved! When it comes to crushing on cute, popular boys I am an *above-average* coward.

Fortunately, Mr. Ono arrives before Drew can

ask me for a kiss under the mistletoe. When he sees what Drew and Henry are up to he says, "I'm glad you found your music for the concert, boys, but I suggest you keep it in your folder, not on top of your head."

Everyone chuckles at Mr. Ono's joke. Drew and Henry smile sheepishly as they put my music back on my stand. Drew gives me a quick grin, then takes off for the percussion section at the back of the room. Henry burps again, then picks up his tuba and sits in the brass section. Everyone quiets down as Mr. Ono steps onto his podium and begins to tell us about our upcoming concert.

"As I mentioned last week, in addition to our band numbers, there will be opportunities for you to play in one of several ensembles, so let me know if you are interested."

Bea and I glance at each other. I can tell we're both thinking the same thing: *Flute duet!*

"Also, I have a big surprise to share with you!"

We look at Mr. Ono again. Then everyone starts

looking around and talking at once, making wild guesses about what the big surprise might be.

"I bet the prez wants us to perform at The White House."

"Maybe Mr. O booked a boy band to come and sing Jingle Bells?"

"I hope the surprise is we get a week off school to practice!"

Mr. Ono waits for everyone to quiet down again before he continues. "Here is the big surprise," he says, holding up a small black instrument case. It looks like my flute case, only it's half the size.

Henry laughs. "I call that a small surprise, Mr. Ono."

"Not as small as your brain," Annelise snarks.

Grace snickers.

Henry frowns. Then he plays a juicy note on his tuba.

"Fffffrrrup!"

He makes a face at Annelise and waves his hand in

front of his freckled nose. "Whoa, Annelise," he says. "Easy on the beans!"

Everyone howls with laughter.

Annelise shoots laser eyes at Henry.

We quiet down again as Mr. Ono opens the case, fitting together the instrument it holds. It looks exactly like my flute, only it's much smaller.

"What is that?" Katie asks from the French Horn section. "The world's smallest flute?"

"It's not a *flute*," Bea pipes in. "It's a piccolo."

"A pickle-*who*?" Henry asks.

Bea rolls her eyes at Henry. "A *piccolo*," she repeats. "It's the smallest woodwind instrument in the band."

"*That's* the big surprise?" Annelise says. She slumps down in her chair. "*Boring.*"

"This is a very special piccolo," Mr. Ono explains. "Just this morning, it was given to our band by a very generous person."

Mr. Ono holds up a letter. We listen as he begins to read it.

Dear Mr. Ono and the members of the Middleton Middle School Band,

When I was a little girl, I couldn't wait to be in the school band. I dreamed of playing the piccolo, but my school didn't have one, and my family did not have a lot of money. My parents owned two instruments — an old clarinet and a dusty trombone. My sister was older than I am, so she got first pick. She chose the clarinet. Even though the trombone wasn't what I wanted to play, I did want to make music with my friends. So I learned how to play it, but I secretly dreamed of playing the piccolo!

I've done many things in my eighty years, but I have never learned to play the piccolo. Now I hope to make my dream come true for someone else! This piccolo is a gift to your band, but I hope you will allow me two requests. First, I would like a front row seat at this year's holiday concert so that I may fully enjoy your performance. Second, I'm asking that the piccolo be featured during one of your songs.

Musically yours,

Mrs. Agnes Petersen

Mr. Ono looks up from reading the letter. "What

do you say?" he asks us. "Shall we grant Mrs. Petersen her wishes?"

"Yes!" we all shout.

"Just don't ask me to play that thing," Henry says. "I'd probably swallow it!"

"The piccolo has the same fingering as the flute," Mr. Ono says. "So the honor will go to someone in our flute section." He looks up and down our row. "Any volunteers?"

Bea's hand shoots up like an arrow. A few other hands go up too, including Jenny's.

Mr. Ono smiles. "I'm happy to see so much interest! It will take extra practice to play the piccolo well in time for the holiday concert."

Jenny bites her lip. "How much extra practice, Mr. Ono?"

Mr. Ono thinks for a moment. "I'd say an hour each night after school. And an extra lesson with me each week."

Jenny's shoulders sag. "I've got gymnastics after

school," she says, lowering her hand.

Other players lower their hands too until only Bea's hand remains in the air.

Even though I'm not the best flute player, I think it's cool that Mrs. Petersen gave the band such a great present. She seems like a nice person. I want to make her wishes come true! But Bea is the best musician around. She could learn to play the piccolo a lot faster and better than me.

Still, the thought of being the *only* piccolo player in the whole Middleton Middle School Band makes my heart race. I can already imagine myself standing at center stage in our school's auditorium, a single spotlight focused on me as I play for Mrs. Petersen and the whole crowd, including my family and friends! Maybe they'd even give me a standing ovation! That would totally make me shine!

I take a deep breath. Then I raise my hand as high as I can.

Mr. Ono looks at me.

Bea looks at me too. Her eyes go wide, like someone just jumped out from nowhere and yelled, "Surprise!"

Quickly, she turns her attention back to Mr. Ono and raises her hand even higher.

But Mr. Ono is still looking at me. "I like your enthusiasm, Vicka!" he says. "And based on your recent flute lessons, I think you have the skill to play this instrument well. All that remains is dedication. Are you willing to practice extra hard over the next few weeks?"

I nod enthusiastically. "Yes, Mr. Ono, I am!"

Mr. Ono smiles again. "Then let's give you first shot at playing the piccolo." He steps down from his podium and places the slender instrument in my hands. It feels as light as a snowflake.

Pling!

Bea's hand falls to her lap.

Wump!

Chapter 3

In a Pickle

"Give it a try, Vicka!" Mr. Ono says encouragingly as he returns to his podium.

I place my fingers on the piccolo's delicate key-pads and hold the mouthpiece to my lips. Then I blow across it, like I do when I'm playing the flute. But instead of a sweet, pretty sound, the note I play is more of wispy wheeze.

Bea clears her throat.

Annelise snorts. "Next!" she says.

Leaning down our row, Bea stretches her hand toward me.

"Here, Vicka," she says, motioning for the piccolo. "Let me try."

But I'm not ready to give up yet. My parents are always saying the only surefire way to fail at something is not to try at all.

I press the instrument to my mouth again and pucker my lips tighter. Then I blow harder.

Screeeaaak!

"Holy cannoli, Vicka!" Henry shouts, clamping his hands over his ears. "Ease up on the pickle, please!"

Everyone laughs.

I cringe, blushing.

But Mr. Ono gives me a look of determination. "Again, Vicka," he says. "Reposition the mouthpiece, pinch your lips, and blow — not hard, not soft, but somewhere in the middle."

Fortunately, I know a lot about being in the middle! I do exactly as Mr. Ono said. This time the note I play is softer and not nearly as screechy. In fact, it's almost pretty!

"That's it, Vicka!" Mr. Ono says. "Keep practicing and you'll be our number one pickle player in no time!"

Everyone laughs again. Katie starts clapping. Grace gives my shoulder a congratulatory pat. Annelise gives me a slight nod. Jenny leans over and gives me a high five. I look down the row at Bea, wanting to share my big moment with her too.

But Bea glances away as soon as I catch her eye. In fact, she doesn't look at me for the rest of band practice.

"You have been chosen!" Henry clamps a hand on my head like The Claw from *Toy Story*. Drew cracks up at Henry as we all leave the band room after practice. "Congrats on getting the part, Vicka," Drew says. "You'll be a great pickle player."

"Thanks!" I reply, ducking out from under Henry's grip and running to catch up with Bea. Usually, we walk to our next class together, but by the time I put away my flute and the piccolo, she's out the door.

"Can you believe Mr. Ono picked me to play the piccolo?!" I say, squeezing Bea's arm excitedly when I finally catch up to her. "I was sure he would pick you."

"Well, he didn't," Bea says, pulling her arm away as she speeds up.

The icy edge to her voice freezes me in my tracks for a moment. "What's the matter?" I ask, catching up to her again by our locker. "Are you upset?"

"No," Bea says, doing the combination on our door lock. "I'm not upset."

"Oh, good!" I say with relief. "Because I was just thinking . . . about our duet? Maybe Mr. Ono would let us play one on flute and piccolo!"

Bea stiffens. Then she lifts up on the door handle. "Um . . . about that," she says, not looking at me. "I think I'm going to be too busy to play a duet with you."

She whips open our locker door so fast it smashes against Henry's locker.

Slam!

Bea switches out notebooks, then briskly walks away, leaving the door hanging open on its hinges.

My mouth hangs open too. Bea never slams things. And she always waits for me so we can walk together to class.

"Brrrrr..." Henry says, pretending to shiver as he walks up behind me. "I hope you brought a sweater today, Vicka."

"Huh?" I reply, looking away from Bea who has just disappeared around the corner. "Why would I need a sweater? It's like an oven in here."

Henry grabs stuff from his locker, then tucks a pencil behind his ear. "I thought you might be cold," he says. "Bea just *iced* you out!"

He wiggles his eyebrows at me, then lopes away.

When I get home from school later, I slip off my backpack, hang up my jacket, and hurry to find Mom. She's in the kitchen with Lucas. He gets home from school earlier than I do because he's only in kindergarten. I tell Mom all about Mr. Ono choosing me to play piccolo for the concert. After Bea's Frosty-the-Snowman imitation, I'm happy for Mom's and Lucas's warm props to my news!

"I like pickles!" Lucas says. "I didn't know you could play one!"

I laugh at my silly little brother. "Lucas, you sound just like Henry! It's called a *piccolo*, not a *pickle*."

"Who's Henry?" Lucas asks.

"The biggest clown in my class," I reply.

Lucas brightens. "I like clowns too!"

"Did you bring the piccolo home?" Mom asks.

I nod and dash to get it from my backpack. "I can't believe Mr. Ono chose me to play it!"

"Why is that a surprise?" Mom asks. "You are a fine flute player."

I put the piccolo together and blow air into the mouthpiece to warm it up. "But Bea is the best flute player. I was sure he would pick her."

"Let's hear what you've got," Mom says.

I've played scales on my flute a zillion times. But when I try to play them now, on the piccolo, the notes sound like squeaks and squawks in our small kitchen.

Lucas covers his ears. "That's one sour pickle!"

Mom shushes my little brother. "Vicka is just learning," she tells Lucas. "Her playing will improve with practice."

Lucas takes a cookie from the package that's sitting on the counter — store-bought since Bea and I didn't have a chance to bake any last weekend. He slips down from the stool he's sitting on. "Let me know when you improve, Vicka," he says, skipping out of the kitchen. "I'll listen then!"

I grimace.

Mom gives me a shoulder hug. "Keep practicing,

Victoria!" she says, encouragingly. "You'll be playing a *sweet* pickle in no time!"

I stick a cookie in my mouth, grab my school stuff, and head upstairs with the piccolo.

I sit on my bed, munch my cookie, and set the piccolo on my nightstand.

Then I stare at it for awhile.

Mom thinks I can shine as the one and only piccolo player at Middleton Middle School.

So does Mr. Ono.

I should be happy, but something is bugging me. For the first time ever, it doesn't feel like my one and only BFF is on my side.

Later, I check my phone for a message from Bea. But the only message there is from Jenny, reminding me to meet up for a chat tonight.

After supper, I find Jenny online. Soon Katie, Grace, and Annelise show up too. But no Bea.

ANNELISE: I have the best idea evah! We're doing an ensemble for the concert! I already told Mr. O.

 JENNY: Who is . . . us?

 ANNELISE: Duh . . . yes.

 JENNY: Oh . . . okay.

 GRACE: Kay!

 KATIE: Kay kay!

 ANNELISE: Vicka? You in?

 VICKA: I'm in. But what about Bea?

 ANNELISE: Already asked her. She said she'd <3 to.

 VICKA: She did? I thought she'd be too busy.

 ANNELISE: Um, no. Why?

45

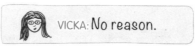 VICKA: No reason.

 ANNELISE: What's up with u 2? Henry said you're fighting.

 JENNY: You are???

 KATIE: I heard that 2.

 GRACE: Me 3.

 VICKA: We're not fighting!

 GRACE: Then why isn't Bea chatting tonight?

 ANNELISE: Cuz she knew V would be here. :p

 VICKA: We're not fighting!

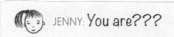 ANNELISE: Uh-huh. Sure. Then how come you were slamming doors? And shouting? Henry said so.

 VICKA: It wasn't like that!

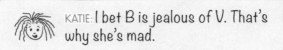

KATIE: I bet B is jealous of V. That's why she's mad.

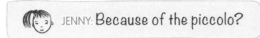

JENNY: Because of the piccolo?

KATIE: Yup.

GRACE: Agreed.

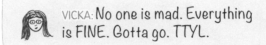

VICKA: No one is mad. Everything is FINE. Gotta go. TTYL.

Even though it's not my bedtime yet, I don't want to get into it with the other girls. I'm sure Bea was just surprised when Mr. Ono didn't pick her. I know I was. Mom and Dad are always saying everything looks brighter in the morning. Bea will probably have forgotten all about the piccolo part by the time I wake up tomorrow. Then everything will be back to normal between us.

Chapter 4

Greensleeves

Instead of everything being bright the next morning, everything is slushy. It's snowing, plus drizzling. A combination my dad calls *snizzling*.

Mom drives us to school so we don't have to trudge through the slush. I try texting Bea to see if she wants a ride, but I don't get a reply. It's not like we go to school together every day — sometimes I'm running late, or she is — but she always replies.

"Hurry up, Vicka," Sofia says, putting on her earmuffs carefully so she doesn't mess up her hair. Sofia was never into hairstyles or makeup until she started liking a boy named Joey Thimble. He lives in our neighborhood. "I have things to do."

"Like what?" I ask. "Lean against your locker and stare at Joey while he stares at you? I've seen you guys. It's gross."

Sofia makes a face. "We're not *staring* at each other. We're discussing important issues that affect our lives."

I roll my eyes at my brainy sister and head out to the car.

"Have a good day!" Mom says later as she drops off Sofia and me in front of the middle school entrance.

"Have a good day!" Lucas adds, mimicking Mom.

As I walk down the sixth-grade wing, I see Bea at our locker. I stop at the water fountain, take a big gulp, apply a fresh layer of Chapstick, and then bop up to her with a cherry-scented smile.

"Hi!" I say very brightly. "How are you today?"

Bea looks at me, then away again. "Oh, hi," she says. "I'm fine."

"That's good!" I reply, sounding as sweet and warm as a freshly toasted Pop Tart. "You didn't text me back, plus you weren't at our chat last night."

"Oh, that," Bea says. "I was busy."

"You can't be *too* busy," I say in a teasey way. "Annelise says you have time to play in our ensemble."

Bea shrugs.

"Which is funny," I continue, "because yesterday you told me you were too busy to play a duet with me."

Bea blows her bangs out of her eyes. "I *am* busy, but I didn't want to be rude," she says — rudely. "So I told Annelise I'd play in *her* group, okay?"

I lean against the lockers, waiting for the bell to ring.

Bea leans and waits too. Neither of us says anything else.

"Keep it down, you guys," Annelise says sarcastically as she walks up to us a minute later. "You'll talk each other's ears off."

"We're just . . . you know . . . thinking about impor-tant issues that affect our lives," I grumble.

Annelise makes a face. "Well, think about this. I just picked out our music for the ensemble! Here it is."

Annelise starts handing out sheet music to Bea and me, then Jenny, Katie, and Grace when they show up a moment later. "It's called 'Greensleeves,'" Annelise tells us. "Isn't that perfect? My concert dress is *green*!"

"But my dress is blue," Grace says.

"Mine is red," Katie adds.

"I'm wearing black pants and a purple sweater," Jenny puts in.

"Then you'll just have to play in the shadows while I stand in the spotlight," Annelise replies.

Bea flips through the "Greensleeves" music. "I played this for my piano recital last year," she says. "It's a good song. We should give it a try."

"See?" Annelise says. "Bea agrees with me. 'Greensleeves' it is!"

I don't know which surprises me more — that Bea is actually speaking or that she was so quick to agree with Annelise's song choice. Normally, she's thumbs down on Annelise's ideas because they usually come with a twist. Not a sweet twist, like an ice cream cone. It's more of an unpleasant twist, like a stomach cramp.

But if Bea is finally acting friendly toward me again, I'm jumping in. "I agree too," I say. "Let's play 'Greensleeves.'"

Annelise nods approvingly. "We'll practice after school today. Meet in the band room."

"I can't," Jenny says. "I have gymnastics after school."

"Oh, darn," Annelise says with fake disappointment. "We'll just have to practice without you."

"That's not fair," I say, sticking up for Jenny. "We all need to practice together — Jenny too."

Annelise sighs as though this is a big inconvenience. "What time are you done?" she asks Jenny.

"Five o'clock," Jenny replies.

Annelise thinks for a moment. "We'll meet at my house instead. Be there at five o'clock, sharp. I'll tell my mother to order pizza."

We all smile because this plan sounds like a party, not like practice!

Even Bea is smiling! I give her a goofy BFF grin and then wait for her to pay it back. But instead, her smile fades when she looks at me. She turns away, sticks "Greensleeves" into her student planner, and takes off for class the moment the bell rings.

We don't have band practice today, but Bea and I have our lesson with Mr. Ono. He has me play the piccolo solo while Bea plays her part on the flute. I'm feeling a little more confident today because I practiced at home last night. I don't sound great, but at least my glasses aren't in danger of shattering!

"Very good, Vicka!" Mr. Ono says at the end of our

lesson. "You have good musicality. You're going to pick up the piccolo quickly!"

I smile happily as Mr. Ono leaves the practice room. I expect Bea to chime in with a compliment too because that's what best friends do. But she just finishes cleaning her flute, puts it back in its case, and snaps the buckles shut.

I'm disappointed, but I'm also determined to stay positive. Trying a new approach, I say, "Do you want to come to my house after school? We could do our homework before going over to Annelise's. Maybe there will be time to work on my piccolo solo too. I could really use your help with it!" Bea loves helping me with stuff. She's the reason I almost made it onto the cheerleading squad!

Bea shakes her head. "I've got stuff to do. I'll meet you at Annelise's house."

I frown. "What *stuff*? Your recital is over. We can do our homework together."

"Just . . . stuff, okay?" Her voice sounds as prickly

as a porcupine. "My world doesn't revolve around you, Victoria."

My breath catches in my throat. "I know that. I just thought it would be fun to hang out."

"Well, it wouldn't be fun," Bea says crisply. "Like I said, I'm busy."

She gathers up her things and heads out, leaving me behind.

I just sit there for a moment, clutching the piccolo like a joystick in the middle of a video battle. Bea and I sometimes disagree on stuff — like pizza toppings and which movies to watch and what the ultimate superpower would be. (I say invisibility, Bea says X-ray vision.) But we always go halfsies or take turns or agree to disagree. We never fight. Not until today.

Dad drives me to Annelise's house later. He's been working a lot lately, so I haven't had a chance to talk to him about getting to play the piccolo. I fill him in on all the details about Mrs. Petersen's letter and how I will make her wish come true by playing a solo at the holiday concert.

"I think I know your Mrs. Petersen!" Dad says. "She stopped in the store on Saturday, asking about piccolos. I didn't know she planned to give it to the school! That was very thoughtful of her."

I nod. "That's why I can't let her down. But I'm worried Mr. Ono made a mistake when he chose me."

"No way," Dad says. "You'll do fine."

I fidget in my seat. "That's what Mr. Ono thinks too. But Bea's mad. She wants the part," I mumble.

"Bea would do fine too," Dad says. "But Mr. Ono gave the part to you. Let's see what you can make of it!"

I give Dad a hug as I get out of the car. I try to smile confidently, even though I'm secretly worried the only thing I will make of the solo is a mess!

When I walk up to Annelise's door a minute later, I paste on my happiest smile. I am determined to be positive and not let the tension between Bea and me get in the way of having a good time with the other girls. Like Dad said, Mr. Ono made his decision. Whether Bea likes it or not, I'm playing the piccolo solo for the concert. If that's too upsetting for her, then I will just have to rely on my other friends for support.

Annelise's mom lets me in and shows me the way to Annelise's room. Even though I've known Annelise since we were little kids, I've only been inside her house a couple of times. The other girls are already there. I set my flute case by their instruments and hop onto the bed with them. It's crowded, but who cares? Bea gives me a slight smile as I plop down next to her. Hooray! Maybe she's done acting like I'm her enemy.

The other girls show me the fancy hairstyles they're looking at in one of the magazines. "We should all get our hair done up for the concert!" Grace says.

"That would be a blast," Katie adds. "We could

do each other's nails too. And take pictures at the concert!"

Everyone thinks this is a fantabulous idea. We all start talking at once, making plans and deciding who is best at manicures, who is best at French braiding hair, and which of us can bring nail polish and extra curling irons.

After a few minutes Bea says, "Don't you guys think we should actually practice our song? We're going to look pretty silly on stage if we're all dressed up, but can't play a note!"

Bea is right, of course. We all hop off the bed and take out our instruments and music.

Annelise glances at me as she puts a new reed on her clarinet. "Vicka, please tell me you're not going to play the piccolo for our ensemble?"

She says this, even though I'm opening my flute case. "Duh," I reply, putting together my flute. "I'm saving the piccolo for my solo."

Annelise sighs dramatically. She loves making a

big deal out of nothing. "Thank goodness," she says. "I want our ensemble to be the best and, no offense, but you sound like an electrified pigeon when you play that piccolo part."

Grace and Katie giggle.

Bea clears her throat, then plays a perfect scale on her flute. She holds out the last note, sweet and clear like a bird song.

Jenny scowls at Annelise. "That was a mean thing to say, Annelise! You owe Vicka an apology."

"I wasn't being mean," Annelise replies. "I was being honest. Vicka is piccolo-challenged. You were at band practice. We all heard how she played."

Grace and Katie exchange glances.

Jenny shakes her head. "No one can learn to play a new instrument in just a few days!"

"Bea could," Annelise snips. "If Mr. Ono had let her try out for the part, we wouldn't have to suffer through 'Sleigh Ride.' Plus, Vicka and Bea wouldn't be fighting."

"We're not fighting," I say. "And thanks for the compliment, Annelise."

Annelise shrugs. "Tough love, Vicka. Bea is better. Everyone knows it."

Jenny growls. "But Mr. Ono didn't give the part to Bea. He gave it to Vicka."

Bea doesn't say anything, but I see her eyes spark for a moment. Like someone, maybe Annelise, just switched on an idea in her head.

"C'mon you guys," Katie says. "Stop arguing. Let's play."

We get busy practicing. When the pizza arrives a few minutes later, we set our instruments aside and dig in. Suddenly, Bea is acting a lot more chummy. She sits next to me when we circle up around the pizza box and even gives me her second breadstick. "You can have it," she says. "I'm stuffed."

I'm stuffed too, but I take the breadstick from her. "Thanks," I say. I'm suspicious, but I'm also happy she's acting like my best friend again.

"How did it go?" Dad asks when he picks me up at Annelise's house.

"It was okay," I say. "We only went through our song a couple times, though, because Annelise, Grace, and Katie kept talking. And then the pizza arrived. We're going to ask Mr. Ono if we can practice during study hall."

"Good plan," Dad says. "No pizza distractions." He's quiet for a moment then asks, "How were things with Bea?"

I don't answer.

"Not so good, eh?" Dad persists.

I sigh. "It's just that everyone knows Bea deserves to play the solo. Annelise even said so."

"What did Bea say?" Dad asks.

"Nothing," I reply. "But she knows it's true. I could see it in her eyes."

"There's no denying Bea is a fine musician," Dad says. "But Mr. Ono saw something in you, or he wouldn't have given you the part." Dad pulls into our driveway and turns off the car. Then he turns toward me. "It's not always about who can play the best notes, Vicka. It's also about who can turn the notes into music. You've got what it takes to do that. Don't shake your head. It's true! I know it. Mr. Ono knows it. Keep practicing, and before long, you'll know it too."

Chapter 5

Worst Day Evah

I hurry to the band room on Wednesday, take the piccolo and my flute out of my cubby, and slip into my chair. I'm nervous about playing with the band today, but I'm excited too. Dad thinks I've got what it takes to play the solo. I'm not going to let him down!

Jenny arrives. She's wearing her favorite blue neck scarf today. It matches her eyes perfectly. "I don't care what Annelise says. I think it's übercool that Mr. Ono chose you to play the piccolo. It's so cute! Can I give it a try?"

"Sure!" I say, handing over the piccolo to Jenny.

She tries playing a few notes, but she can barely make a sound. *"Ohmygosh!"* she says, handing the piccolo back to me. "I thought it would be easy, but that's really hard to play! I'm glad I backed out."

When Mr. Ono arrives, I take the piccolo back and sit up straight and tall in my chair. My eyes follow Bea as she slips into her chair. Usually, she is the first one here, but today she is the last to arrive.

"Let's begin with 'Sleigh Ride,'" Mr. Ono says to everyone. "I want Vicka to try her piccolo part. She will play the melody line at measure forty-three while the band provides background harmony. Our job is to support the melody without overpowering it." He looks over our flute section. "But first, we'll need a new seating arrangement. Bea, will you please give Vicka your chair? I'd like to have the piccolo at the end of the row."

Bea's mouth drops open. "But, *I'm* first chair, Mr. Ono," she says.

Mr. Ono nods. "You'll still be first chair of the flute

section, Bea," he says. "But now we need a piccolo chair too."

I stand up, and the other girls scoot down, filling in. Reluctantly, Bea slides down one chair too. I take her place in the first chair.

Mr. Ono raises his baton. "Let's take it from the top!" He looks at me. "Ready, Vicka?"

I fidget, partly because I'm nervous and partly because it feels like the air around Bea is crackling. "I think so," I reply.

The band begins playing. I count measures until it's time for me to come in.

Mr. Ono points his baton at me and nods. I start playing, just like I practiced at my lesson yesterday, but only Bea and Mr. Ono were there then. Today it's the whole band. The music isn't hard, but my first few notes blast out of the piccolo. I hear Annelise groan behind me. I keep playing, but with everyone listening to me, the notes sputter from the piccolo like a lawn mower that's almost out of gas. Then I lose my place in the music. I lean toward Bea. "What measure are we on?" I ask her.

But either Bea doesn't hear me, or she's ignoring me. She leans into her music and plays her part louder than ever.

"Softer, Bea," Mr. Ono calls out as he conducts. "Help Vicka find her spot."

Bea stops playing and quickly pokes a finger at my music. "There," she says and starts playing her flute again.

"*Where?*" I ask, feeling frantic. All the notes look like pepper sprinkled on the page.

"*There!*" she says again, pointing. This time she pokes the music hard. My stand wobbles back and forth. My music slips off and falls to the floor.

Bea keeps playing.

I scramble to pick it up then jump back into the song. But my notes don't match what everyone else is playing. I'm completely lost.

Mr. Ono brings the band to a stop. "Good first try,

Vicka," he says brightly. "Let's give you a few more days to practice on your own. We'll try your part with the band again on Friday. For now, everyone take out 'Still, Still, Still.'"

I set the piccolo on my lap. It feels as heavy as a tuba.

"Thank goodness," I hear Annelise whisper to Grace over the rustle of paper as everyone shifts to the new song. "That was a train wreck!"

"Word," Grace whispers back. "I wonder if Mr. Ono regrets giving her the part?"

"I would," Annelise replies.

My eyes sting with tears. I try to blink them away. I don't want to cry in front of everyone. That would be worse than the time I threw up in first grade. Henry still calls me Sicka sometimes. I don't want him to call me Cry Baby too.

I glance at Bea. Did she hear what Annelise and Grace just said? If she did, she's not coming to my defense. The thought of Bea agreeing with them makes my eyes sting even more. Like someone just threw a slushball that hits me right in the face.

Long after band practice, my ears are *still, still, still* ringing with Annelise's and Grace's comments. I held in my tears all afternoon. Finally, the last bell rings, and I can't wait to grab my stuff from my locker and cry all the way home. This has been one of my most unfortunately awful days *evah*. The only good thing about it is that it couldn't get any worse. The piccolo may be the smallest instrument in our band, but right now it feels like my biggest problem.

"You played great today, Vicka!" Jenny tells me as everyone rushes to catch a bus or get to sports practice.

I try to give Jenny an upbeat smile, but what I really want to do is crawl inside my locker and wait until everyone has left. "Thanks," I tell Jenny, "but I feel like such a loser. I totally messed up."

"I think you're brave to play a new instrument," Jenny tells me. "I didn't even want to try."

"But what if I can't pull it off? I'll be a total disappointment to Mrs. Petersen." I pause, biting my lip and weighing my options. "Maybe I should let Bea play the solo. I know she could play it perfectly. She deserves the part more than me."

"Wrong answer," Jenny says. "You can't quit after just one try! Our next rehearsal isn't until Friday. You'll have lots of time to practice before then. It will go much better. Wait and see!" Jenny gives me an encouraging hug, then heads out.

Just then, Bea arrives at our locker. I can't help it, now that Jenny got me talking, I can't stop. "I was a total flop today!" I blurt out. "Bea, you have to help me master the piccolo or I'll never shine in time for the concert!"

I expect Bea to give me a sympathetic hug or at least a pep talk, like Jenny did. Instead, she glares at me. "You're not the only one who wants to *shine*, you know. I hope you and my chair are very happy together."

I take a step back, blown away by the bitterness in Bea's voice.

Bea punches her fists into her hips. "Why did you even raise your hand?" she persists. "You knew I wanted the part."

"I wanted it too!" I say, coming to my own defense.

Bea shakes her head at me. "No, you didn't. The only thing you wanted was to be in the spotlight." She crosses her arms. "You think playing the piccolo will make you shine, but it won't. Only playing it *well* can do that."

I lock eyes with Bea. "I *want* to play it well! That's what I've been trying to tell you. But you won't help me. Ever since Mr. Ono gave the part to me, you won't even talk to me!"

"I'm talking to you now," Bea says. "I don't have anything to prove by playing the piccolo."

"I'm not trying to prove anything!" I shout. "I just

want to play the solo well and make Mrs. Petersen's wishes come true."

"SO. DO. I!" Bea shouts back.

A few kids who are still in the hall glance over at us. Bea's eyes fill with angry tears.

So do mine.

"I don't want to fight with you," I say just above a whisper. "But Mr. Ono gave the part to *me*. Nothing can change that."

Bea rubs a tear from her cheek. "One thing can," she says.

I stare blankly at Bea. "What?"

Bea doesn't answer. She just grabs her backpack and takes off without saying another word.

I was wrong. This *is* my most unfortunately awful day *evah*.

Chapter 6

A Change of Plans

I'm done crying by the time I get home later, but Mom can still tell that something is wrong. She's like a satellite dish that way, picking up signals on how I'm feeling as soon as I enter the room.

I spill the whole story to her. "Mr. Ono made Bea give her chair to me, so now she's jealous that I get to sit at the end of the row," I tell Mom. "Instead of being happy for me, she's super mad and feeling sorry for herself. She'll barely even talk to me! And when she does, her voice is sharper than a porcupine. Today when I asked her to help me with my piccolo solo, she went bonkers! She told me I only want the part so I can be in the spotlight."

Fresh tears spring to my eyes. I take a quivery breath. "She makes it sound like I'm being selfish for wanting the part. But she's the selfish one!"

Mom hands me a tissue. I take off my glasses, wipe my eyes, and blow my nose while she thinks things through. "It must have come as a real shock to Bea, not to get the part."

"I suppose, but Mr. Ono said I have what it takes to play the piccolo well. Dad even agreed. He told me Mr. Ono wouldn't have chosen me if he didn't think I could make the solo special."

"I don't doubt it," Mom says, "and I'm proud of you for volunteering. But music is everything to Bea. She works at it very hard. I can see why she would be upset, not to be chosen for the part. And giving up her chair? That must have stung too."

My eyes go wide, and my mouth drops open. Even my mom is against me!

"It sounds like you're taking her side," I say.

Mom shakes her head. "I'm not taking sides. I'm just looking at the situation from both angles. Bea is an accomplished musician and the top flute player in the band. She had the furthest to fall when the rug was pulled out from under her."

"But —" I start to say.

Mom raises her hand, quieting me. "Give Bea some time. She'll pick herself up and dust herself off again. You've been friends too long to let something like this come between you."

Ever since our big blow up on Wednesday, I've tried to keep my distance from Bea. Mom said I should be patient and give her time to get over the shock of not getting the solo, so I skated around her as much as possible yesterday. But it's hard to totally avoid someone you share a locker with. We don't talk, but we shoot lots of glances at each other. News spreads fast in this school. Everyone heard about our fight. The other girls keep looking at us in a worried way. Even Annelise is being nicer to me. She came with me yesterday when I got a study hall pass to the band room to practice my solo. We worked on "Greensleeves" for a while too. Afterward she gave me one of her stretchy bracelets to wear. She said it was because it matched my outfit, but I think it was mostly because she knows I'm feeling bad.

Today is Friday, so I decide to end the week on a positive note. I wait at the corner on my way to school, but no Bea. Taking out my phone, I type a message to her.

> I'm at the corner. R U coming? Sorry things have been a little crazy lately.

A moment later my phone buzzes.

Score!

A message from Bea.

> Go without me.

I make a puzzled face and tap out another message.

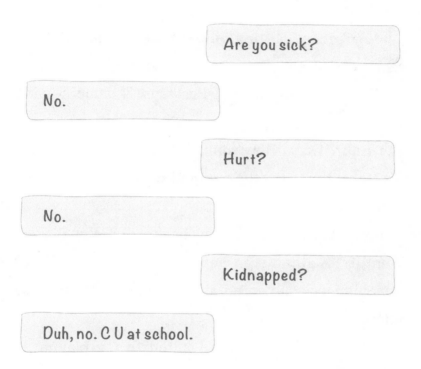

Are you sick?

No.

Hurt?

No.

Kidnapped?

Duh, no. C U at school.

Tucking the phone in my pocket, I head down the sidewalk alone. There are lots of footprints in the snow as I get to school, but today it feels like there is only one pair. Mine, minus Bea's.

I go straight to the band so I can stash the piccolo before first hour. But, much to my surprise, I nearly topple Bea, who is coming out of the instrument room just as I'm going in.

"*¡Ay!*" I say, putting on the brakes. "How did you beat me to school?"

"I was here all along," Bea says. "I came in early today."

"Huh?" I say. "How come?"

"I wanted to try the piccolo," she says. "But I guess you took it home last night."

I nod and take it out of my backpack. "Why did you want it?" A glimmer of hope shimmers in me. "Have you changed your mind about helping me learn my part?"

"No," Bea says. "I just wanted to try playing it. That's all." Bea glances at a clock on the wall. "The bell is going to ring. Better hurry or we'll be late for history."

Bea heads out. It isn't until lunchtime that she slows down long enough for me to talk to her.

Seeing her by the milk cooler, I grab my lunch and

walk over. "Hi!" I say as cheerfully as I can. "I haven't seen you all morning. Where have you been?"

"Around," Bea says, picking through the cartons of milk, looking for chocolate.

"Do you want to come over this weekend? We haven't hung out, just the two of us, for so long. I promise I won't mention the pic—" I stop myself before I can say the word *piccolo*. "Jenny mentioned getting together again to practice our ensemble."

"Maybe," she says, "But —"

Drew walks up to us. "Hi, Vicka. Hey, you're doing a great job on the piccolo. I've been meaning to tell you that."

"Thanks," I say, looking from Drew to Bea. For the first time ever, I'm wishing he wasn't here. I really want to finish this conversation with my BFF.

Drew turns to Bea. "Hey, Bea, I've been looking for you. Mr. Ono told me that you play piano?"

Bea nods. "I've been taking piano lessons since I was three."

"Cool," Drew says. "Henry and I are doing a tuba and drum duet for the concert. There's a piano part too. Mr. Ono suggested I ask you to accompany us. What do you say?"

Bea gasps like someone just offered her whipped cream on her chocolate milk. "I'd love to!" she exclaims.

"Great!" Drew says. He takes some music out of the folder he's carrying. "I've got a drum set. We have a piano too. Henry's bringing his tuba home for the weekend. We could practice at my house on Saturday, if you're free."

Bea's eyes go wide. "I'm totally free," she says. "Saturday would be perfect!"

My eyes go wide too. Drew is the most popular boy in our class. Bea is an average girl, like me. Neither of us has ever been invited to hang out at his house. We haven't been invited to hang out at any boy's house, unless you count relatives.

"Give me your digits," Drew says to Bea, taking out his phone. "I'll text you later with the time."

Bea sets down her tray and takes out her phone too. I can see that her hands are shaking as she adds Drew's number to her contacts.

Grrr!

Drew is my crush, but he's never asked me for my phone number.

Bea waves good-bye as Drew leaves the Caf. "See you on Saturday!" she calls after him.

I give Bea the stink eye. "You said you were too busy to come over to my house this weekend. Now you have time to hang out with Drew and Henry?"

"We're not hanging out," Bea says, stretching her neck to watch as Drew disappears from the Caf. "I'm helping Drew with his duet. That's different."

Bea tucks the piano music under her arm, sets her phone on her lunch tray, and carries it to a table.

"What about our ensemble?" I persist. "We need to practice that too."

"Don't worry," she replies as we sit down to eat. "I already know how to play 'Greensleeves' on the piano. I'm sure it won't take me long to learn the flute part."

She clicks her phone, checking for messages. Does she think Drew is texting her already? *¡Uf!* Usually Bea doesn't pay attention to boys unless it's to tell them to stop acting like Neanderthals. But now that Drew has invited her to his house, she is suddenly boy crazy. I just wish she was crazy about someone else's crush, not mine.

Bea is fluttering around school all afternoon. No lie, I actually saw her skipping down the hallway, like Lucas does when Dad lets him stay up past his bedtime to play video games. I swear, her feet weren't even touching the tile. I guess getting an invitation to Drew's house gives you superpowers.

Setting the piccolo and my flute on my lap at band practice, I take "Sleigh Ride" from my folder. I try playing my part while everyone is busy talking and warming up their instruments. I always seem to play better when I'm not in the spotlight.

Bea breezes in and sits down next to me.

"Hi, Vicka!" she says.

"Hi, Bea," I reply, surprised by her friendliness. "I looked for you at study hall, but you weren't there."

"Oh, I got a pass from Mr. Ono. I was here, in the band room, practicing."

"Is the piano part hard?" I ask.

Bea makes a face. "What piano part?"

"The one you are playing with Drew and Henry. Isn't that what you were practicing?"

"Oh!" Bea says. "No. The accompaniment is easy. I was practicing something else."

Just then, Mr. Ono steps onto his podium. "We have a great variety of ensembles lined up for our holiday concert! And, of course, our new piccolo will be featured in our grand finale number." He pauses to look at me, then at Bea. "And since we have two flutists who are eager to play the solo, I've decided the fair thing to do is hold an audition."

Bea smiles.

I gawk. "But Mr. Ono," I say, raising my hand, "I thought *I* was playing the piccolo for the concert?"

"That was my original plan, Vicka," Mr. Ono replies. "But Bea spoke with me earlier and has challenged you to an audition! You will both have a week to practice. The winner of the audition will play the solo at the concert. I think it will motivate both of you to practice and do your best!"

My chin practically drops to my knees. This morning, I was the star piccolo player in the band. Now I'm competing against the best musician in the band for the part!

"Since you've already tried the part with the band, Vicka, let's give Bea a turn today." Mr. Ono says.

"But —" I start to complain.

Bea smiles and gets up from her chair. She holds out her hand, waiting for me to give her the piccolo.

Grrr! I hand it over, then scoot down.

"Let's begin at measure thirty," Mr. Ono tells us. "Bea, you come in at measure forty-three."

Bea nods. "Yes, Mr. Ono, I remember from our last practice when I had to help Vicka find her place in the music."

I give Bea a superdeluxe stink eye.

A minute later, Bea's fingers are flying over the piccolo keys like hummingbird wings. I guess her new superpower applies to playing the piccolo too. She barely makes any mistakes. This must be what she was practicing during study hall!

"Nicely done, Bea!" Mr. Ono says when we come to the end of the song. "Since we have only one piccolo, you and Vicka will need to take turns bringing it home to practice. Who would like to have it this weekend?"

"Vicka can," Bea says. "I'm practicing with Drew and Henry tomorrow anyway." Bea shoots a smile in Drew's direction. He smiles back.

Chapter 7

Cookie Chaos

Now that Bea has challenged me to an audition, she's acting like my best buddy again. She texted me a zillion times on Saturday — before, during, and after practicing at Drew's house. She said Drew is just as nice out of school as in school and that Henry is actually more funny than annoying. He got her laughing so hard, she hiccupped for an hour! They're even making plans to form their own band!

I offered to bring the piccolo to her house on Sunday so she could practice the solo, but Bea said she was busy trying to find a lead singer and guitar player. Plus, she, Drew, and Henry were brainstorming band names. So far they'd come up with Drew and the Dropouts, Out of Tuna, and The Marginal Toasters.

I practiced so much over the weekend that I'm really getting good at my part. Today at band, Annelise only groaned two times when we practiced "Sleigh Ride," and afterward, I overheard Henry say to his buddies, "Hey, I hardly cringed at all that time."

Even Bea, just now, paid me a compliment as we switch out our music. She said, "I liked the way you added that trill at the end of measure fifty. Do you mind if I do that too?"

Dad thinks imitation is the highest form of flattery. He tells me this when Lucas is following me around all day, aping everything I do. I much prefer my BFF copying me than my little brother.

"Of course not!" I reply. Bea and I exchange smiles. "Do you want to come over after school? We could study for our math quiz."

Bea thinks for a moment. She's just about to answer me when Mr. Ono calls for everyone's attention. "We'll see lots of activity around here starting this week. The Booster Club will begin decorating the auditorium with lots of glitter and greenery. They could use your help stringing up lights, decorating trees, and hanging garlands. Please add your name to the sign-up sheet if you can lend a hand. Ensemble players, make sure you're finding time to practice. Let me know if you need study hall passes to come to the band room. Oh, and Bea? Vicka? We'll hold your audition for the piccolo solo on Friday during band. That way, the winner will have time to play with us before the concert the following Saturday."

Bea raises her hand. "Mr. Ono, did you say the audition will be during band?"

"Yes," he replies. "Everyone will vote for their favorite performance."

Bea gapes at Mr. Ono. "The whole band decides the winner, not just you?"

"Correct!" Mr. Ono says. "We'll put it to a vote." He smiles down at us. "May the best pickle win!"

Bea slumps back in her chair. She blows her bangs and crinkles her forehead, which means she's thinking hard about something.

"What about studying after school?" I say again. "Do you want to?"

"Um . . ." Bea says, the gears still turning inside her head. I can practically hear them. "I can't. There's something very important I have to do."

I frown, puzzled. "What is it?" I ask.

"Um . . . er . . ." Bea says, hesitantly. "I can't tell you. It's a surprise."

The next morning, my locker smells like a cookie factory. When I open the door, it looks like one too. Cookie containers are stacked as high as my coat hook. "What's going on?" I ask, glancing at Jenny. She's standing by her locker, munching a cookie.

"Bea baked cookies last night," Jenny explains. "I helped her carry them in from her Mom's car. She said she wanted to do something nice for everyone!"

I turn and watch as Bea walks up and down the hall with a cookie container in her hand and a smile on her face, offering cookies to almost everyone she sees.

A moment later, Bea hurries back to our locker with her empty cookie container.

"Oh! Hi, Vicka! Surprise!" she says, taking a new container of cookies out of our locker and tossing the empty container in. "Help yourself — I made choco- late chip, peanut butter, and oatmeal raisin!"

I frown. Not that I don't like cookies. I do. But something smells fishy about this batch.

"How come you've turned into the Keebler elf?" I ask.

Bea laughs lightly. "I like to bake, that's all! And everyone loves cookies." She turns and holds out the container to Henry and three of his buddies — two of them play in the brass section. The third, Tony, sings in choir.

Bea pulls the container away as Tony reaches for a cookie. "Um . . . you're not in band, are you?" she says to him.

"Nope," Tony replies. "Choir."

Bea shakes her head, sympathetically. "Sorry, but I'm running short," she tells Tony. "Band members only." Then she slips away before Tony can complain.

A moment later, she approaches two girls who play saxophone. "Would you like some cookies? I baked them myself. Take as many as you want!"

The girls dig in. "Thanks, Bea!" one of them says.

"Yeah, you've got my vote!" the other one adds, giving Bea a high five.

Bea beams. "Thanks!" she calls out as the girls walk away, chowing down on their cookies.

"I'm impressed," I hear someone say. Turning, I see Annelise leaning against the lockers, watching everyone swarm around Bea, eating cookies by the dozen.

"Bea is sneakier than I thought. I've been watching her for a while now. She's only giving cookies to band members. She's trying to buy votes before the piccolo audition."

Okay, so I'm not a total dunce. The thought already crossed my mind, but I didn't let it settle in because Bea is my BFF. I always try to think the best of her. But now that Annelise has said it, there's no ignoring the fact that my best friend has a sneaky side, and it's working against me today.

"What are you going to do about it?" Annelise asks me.

I shrug. "Auditions are on Friday. If I bring cookies too, everyone will call me a copycat. Besides, if I spend all my time baking cookies, I won't have time to practice my solo. All I can do is keep working on my part and hope I play better than her."

"Wrong answer," Annelise says. "For one thing, you will never play better than Bea. For another thing, you will never, ever play better than Bea."

I make a face. "Thanks."

Annelise tightens her ponytail. "You need something better than a batch of cookies if you're going to beat Bea."

"Like what?" I ask.

Annelise's lips curl into a Grinchy grin. "A rumor," she replies, pulling me aside. "If you spread a bad rumor about Bea, kids will think twice about voting for her."

"I can't do that!" I exclaim.

Annelise purses her lips and rolls her eyes. "Don't be such a goody-goody, Vicka," she says. "You want to win the audition, don't you?"

I square my shoulders. "Yes. But Bea is my best friend. I'm not going to tell lies about her."

Annelise thinks for a moment. Then she grins again. "Bea isn't *my* best friend. I'll do it."

Before I can say another word, Annelise walks over to the crowd gathered around Bea. "I'm sorry," Bea keeps telling them as they beg for cookies. "I only have enough for band members. Think about joining!"

"Yoo-hoo, Bea!" Annelise waves. "I'm in band. May I have a cookie?"

Bea sees Annelise waving and smiles brightly. "Of course, Annelise! Which kind would you like? Chocolate chip, peanut butter, or oatmeal raisin?"

"Oatmeal raisin, please," Annelise says politely.

Bea pushes through the crowd and gives Annelise an oatmeal raisin cookie. "Would you like two?" she asks.

"No, thank you," Annelise says taking a big bite out of the cookie. "One will be plenty." She walks away, munching.

Annelise waits until Bea goes back to work, hunting down band members and handing out cookies. Then she looks at her half-eaten cookie, makes a horrified face, and runs over to the water fountain where a group of older girls from band are talking.

Annelise makes a big deal of throwing the cookie

into a trash can. Then she starts gulping water at the fountain.

The girls stop talking and look at her. "What's the matter?" one of them asks. "Don't you like cookies?"

Annelise straightens up, wiping water from her chin. "Not when they have *bugs* in them," she replies.

"Bugs?!" the girls cry out.

Annelise nods. "At first I thought they were *raisins*. But then I saw *legs*. And *wings*!" Annelise shudders. "I think I swallowed one!"

One of the girls gasps. "I ate two of Bea's cookies!" she says.

Another one clutches her stomach. "I ate *three!*"

Annelise shakes her head with fake concern. "I'm sure they weren't *poisonous* bugs. But you might want to see the school nurse. Just don't tell anyone where you got the cookies, okay? Bea is one of my best friends. I don't want people to know she fed them bugs."

But the girls are already halfway down the hall,

stopping kids along the way, talking a mile a minute and pointing back toward Bea.

Annelise walks up to me again, dusting off her hands. "And that's the way the cookie crumbles," she says smugly.

By the end of lunch hour, Annelise's rumor has spread through the entire school. Instead of begging Bea for cookies, kids are wiggling their fingers over their head like bug feelers when she walks by. Jokes follow her from classroom to classroom.

"Does anyone have dental floss? I've got a bug wing stuck in my tooth."

"Bea, those caterpillar chip cookies were delicious. Can I get the recipe?"

"Knock, knock. Who's there? Bea. Bea who? Bea careful what you eat!"

"Buzz . . .buzz . . . buzz . . ." Henry says, flapping his arms like bug wings and circling Bea as she tries to get past him in the hallway. "Boy, I could sure go for some honey. Got any, *Bee*? Or is your name short for *Bea*tle? Do your parents love insects or something?"

Henry laughs good-naturedly and punches Bea's shoulder like they are old buddies, but Bea's face turns ladybug red. She bolts away, laughter and bug jokes following her down the hall. I don't see her again until it's time for our lesson with Mr. Ono. But Bea's mind is not on her playing. When it's her turn to practice the piccolo part, she stumbles over the notes and finally asks Mr. Ono if she can be excused to the girls' room. With tears in her eyes, she dashes out.

"Oh, dear!" Mr. Ono exclaims. "The pressure of auditioning must be getting to Bea. I was sure she could handle it."

"She can, Mr. Ono," I say. "It's not the audition that's bugging Bea."

"What then?" he asks.

"Some of the other kids didn't like the cookies she baked. That's all." I've never fibbed to a teacher before, but if I tell Mr. Ono the real reason Bea is upset, he might blame me for the rumor. He might even disqualify me from auditioning for the piccolo part. I keep quiet.

I look for Bea in the hallway later but only catch a glimpse of her between classes.

After school, I think about calling Bea, but what would I say? That I know the rumor isn't true? If I tell her that, she'll think I had something to do with it and that will make things even worse between us. Besides, she did try to buy votes by giving band kids cookies. That was a sneaky thing to do. And the rumor does seem to be working.

I set down my phone again. Maybe things will be better tomorrow without me saying anything.

Chapter 8

Beatle

Unfortunately, things are not better the next day. When I get to our locker, someone has taped a fly swatter to it! I tear it down just as Bea arrives.

She looks at me, standing there with a fly swatter in my hand, and then gives me a deadly squint. "Is that your idea of a joke?" she asks. "Bringing a fly swatter to school?"

"It's not mine!" I say. "I found it when I got here."

Bea huffs like she doesn't believe me, opens our locker, tosses in her stuff, then bolts away. I toss the fly swatter into the trash can by the water fountain.

When it's time for lunch, Jenny catches up with me. "Hey, I've got something for you, Vicka," she says as we head into the Caf. She unwinds her pretty blue neck scarf and gives it to me. "It's my favorite, so I thought it might bring you good luck at your audition!"

I take the scarf from Jenny and put it on. "Thanks!" Holding up my hands like I'm playing a piccolo I ask, "How do I look?"

"Fantabulous!" Jenny says. "I can't wait to see you play for real. You and Bea will both do great!"

Jenny and I get our food and sit at a table with Annelise, Grace, and Katie. I look around the Caf, but I can't see Bea anywhere. Maybe she brought a cold lunch today so she could avoid a crowd of teasers during lunchtime.

Annelise eyes up the scarf I'm wearing. "What's that around your neck, Vicka?" she asks. "Some sort of bug netting?" She laughs at her own joke. Grace snickers too.

"Aren't you afraid to share a locker with Bea?" Katie asks me. "If you aren't careful, you'll need an exterminator!"

"You don't really believe that silly rumor, do you?" I say to Katie.

"What makes you think it's a rumor?" Grace cuts in. "Do you know who started it?" She glances at Annelise.

A grin whisks across Annelise's face. She stabs a tater tot with her fork.

"No," I reply.

But Jenny doesn't buy my fib. She looks at Annelise. "You started the cookie rumor, didn't you," she says matter-of-factly.

Annelise puts a hand to her chest. "Who, me?" she says innocently. Then she pops another tater tot into her mouth.

I duck my head and dig into my mac and cheese, wishing I'd stopped Annelise before she mentioned the word *bug*. But I didn't. And now I'm stuck with feeling like a total jerk for letting the rumor get out of hand.

Sitting next to Bea at band practice later, I try to act like everything is normal, even though two eighth grade girls just elbowed each other as they walked by us saying, "Isn't that the girl everyone is calling Beatle?"

Bea cringes and sinks down in her chair.

My stomach churns. I should say something to everyone before Mr. Ono gets here. I could tell them that rumor isn't true and that I'm responsible for letting it spread.

That's what I *should* do.

Instead, I sink down in my chair too, feeling lower than a flea on Poco's belly. Doing nothing to stop a rumor is just as bad as starting one.

"Did you hear about the solo Bea is playing for the concert?" Annelise says to Grace as they take their seats behind Bea and me. "It's called 'Flight of the Bumblebee'!"

Grace cracks up.

Bea clutches the piccolo on her lap. It's her turn to play it today.

"Don't listen to them," I whisper to her. "I've baked cookies with you lots of times. I know the rumor isn't true."

Bea zeros in on me. "Do you know who started it?"

My skin prickles from the heat of Bea's glare. I wonder if this is how a snowman feels just before it melts. "Um . . ." I say. "Maybe it was one of the boys? It seems like something Henry would do."

Now I feel lower than a flea on Poco's toenail! Not only did I let a rumor about my best friend get out of hand, now I've blamed it on someone else!

For the rest of band practice, I keep my eyes on my music. I sit up straight and play with gusto, like Mr. Ono is always reminding us to do. But secretly, I'm sneaking glances at Bea and feeling like our friendship is a giant Jenga tower. If one more block gets shifted, the whole thing is going to crash to the ground.

When Bea and I are getting our stuff together at the end of the day, Drew appears by our locker. "Hey, Bea," he says. "I'm starving. Do you have any more cookies?"

Bea stiffens. "Very funny," she says.

But Drew just smiles. "Really," he says. "They were the best cookies I've ever eaten, and if you have any more, I'll take one for the road."

Bea relaxes a little when she realizes Drew isn't joking. "I threw the rest away," she says. "Haven't you heard? Some people think there were bugs in them." She shoots a look at me.

Drew lifts a shoulder. "Can't believe everything you hear. Henry and I are staying after school to practice. You in?"

Bea doesn't answer right away. "That depends," she finally says. "Did Henry start the rumor?"

"What?!" Drew says. "No way. Henry's a goofball, but he's not a jerk. Besides, I think he likes you."

Bea blinks. "He does?"

Drew nods. "Yeah, every time I mention your name his face lights up like a railroad crossing."

Bea ducks her head, blushing.

"See you later?" Drew asks.

Bea smiles. "Okay, I'll be there," she tells him. Then she pauses. "But I won't bring cookies."

Drew laughs. "Darn!" he says, giving Bea a grin.

"He's so nice," she says as Drew catches up to a couple of buddies and starts talking with them. "I can't decide who I like more . . . Drew or Henry."

I zip up my puffy coat. "Do you want to take the piccolo home?" I ask, picking up the case. "You really should practice too, you know."

"Hmm?" Bea says, looking at me like she forgot I was there. "Did you say something?"

"I said, do you want to take the piccolo home? To practice? The audition is on Friday, in case you've forgotten." I say that last part in a sassy voice, because I'm not crazy about the way Bea is stretching her neck to watch Drew as he talks with his friends.

"No, you can take it home," she replies. "I'm going to be busy practicing with Drew and Henry tonight."

"But I've taken it home almost every night for the past week," I say. "No offense, Bea, but you didn't play that great at our last lesson."

Bea brushes off my comment. "I was just upset about the cookie rumor. I'm fine now. Do you think what Drew said is true? That *Henry* likes me?" She laughs to herself, then looks at Drew again. "Gotta go. See you tomorrow."

Catching up to Drew, she taps him and the shoulder. He turns and smiles at her. Then they walk toward the band room together.

I grab my homework and close my locker door. *Slam!*

The sound echoes down the hallway like the whole school is about to come crashing down.

I toss and turn half the night, thinking about what's been happening at school lately. It's like my brain is playing a game of Ping-Pong with my heart. First, Bea tried to get in good with all the band members by passing out cookies. *Ping!* Then everyone turned against her because of the rumor Annelise started. *Pong!* Then I pretended I didn't know anything about how the rumor got started. *Ping!* Then Drew took Bea's side, which made her go gaga over *my* crush. *Pong!* She's probably dreaming about him right now.

I crawl out of bed and find my piccolo. Poco looks up from the foot of my bed where he likes to sleep. But it's late and he's tired, so a moment later he's snoozing again.

I practiced my solo earlier, but I feel like playing it again now.

Even though it's dark in my room, I close my eyes and play my solo by heart. I can't remember all of it, but I keep going, making up my own song. Dad calls that improvisation. He says being able to play improv is the mark of a real musician. As I keep playing, I realize the notes aren't coming from a sheet of music, they are coming from me.

I play and play, thinking about Bea. If I tell her the truth about the rumor, will she forgive me or hate me? I play louder and faster as I imagine Bea walking away from me, my fingers pounding the keys. My heart pounds against my chest.

Then I hear more pounding, only it's not coming from my fingers or my heart. It's coming from my sister's bedroom.

Pound! Pound! Pound!

"Victoria Torres!" Sofia shouts as she bangs on the wall that separates our rooms. "It's the middle of the night! Stop playing that thing!"

I set down the piccolo, hop back into bed, and pull

Poco closer to me. Even though I've practiced my solo a zillion times in the past couple of weeks, tonight it feels like I really played it for the very first time.

Chapter 9

Audition Day

As I get ready for school on Friday morning, I tie on the blue scarf Jenny let me borrow. Even though she said it will bring me good luck, I know it will take more than that for me to win the audition today. Bea has been off her mark lately, but she is still the best musician in our band. Still, playing improv on the piccolo last night made me feel better than my best. I want to play like that again — the notes weren't perfect, but the music was.

I put the piccolo into my backpack and head off to school. When I get to the corner, I look down the street toward Bea's house. A puffy pink marshmallow is approaching me. I know it's Bea. I have her walk memorized. Do I wait for her to catch up or don't I? Should I wish her good luck on the audition?

Suddenly Bea stops, takes out her phone, and looks at the screen. She must have gotten a message from someone. Drew, maybe?

I turn and walk off.

At band practice later, Mr. Ono greets Bea and me from his podium. "Are you girls ready for your audition?"

"Yes," we both reply.

"Good," Mr. Ono says. "We'll hold it first, then the winner may practice the piccolo solo with the whole band." He looks toward the back of the room. "Drew and Henry? Would you hand out ballots while Bea and Vicka get situated in the practice room?"

Drew and Henry come forward and take a stack of scratch paper from Mr. Ono.

"Mr. Ono?" I say, raising my hand. "I think I've practiced all I can. I don't need to go to the practice room."

"Same for me, Mr. Ono," Bea puts in. "I'd rather just do the audition now."

"Oh, I'm sorry, girls," Mr. Ono says. "I should have explained. We will hold blind auditions for the part."

Henry looks up from handing out scratch paper. "Blind auditions?" he says. "Does that mean Bea and Vicka have to wear blindfolds?"

"No," Mr. Ono replies. "Bea and Vicka may look at their music, but the band will not be able to see who is playing. The votes will be based on skill only. That will make the audition completely fair."

Annelise mumbles something about blind auditions and cookies. Then I hear her say, "A perfectly good rumor gone to waste."

Bea turns quickly and gives Annelise a sharp look. Then she picks up her music and marches to the practice room.

I follow along.

Mr. Ono joins us a moment later, handing each of us a folded slip of paper. "Even I won't know who is playing."

When he rejoins the band, I unfold my slip of paper.

Bea will play first.

"Musician #1?" Mr. Ono calls out. "We're ready when you are!"

Bea takes a deep breath, then sets her music on a stand while I sit off to the side. She begins to play. I can tell she is counting carefully and playing each note the best she can. Still, her fingers stumble. And the song sounds rushed, like she wants to get it over with. She plays well, but I know it's not her best even before her shoulders sag at the end of the solo.

Everyone applauds politely. Then I switch places with Bea, looking at the music she left on the stand. I remember how it felt to play with no music last night.

"Whenever you're ready, Musician #2!" Mr. Ono calls out.

I put the piccolo to my lips, close my eyes, and begin to play. I don't play every note exactly right, but I play the whole piece by heart. When I get to the end, I open my eyes and smile. Even if I don't win the audition, I know I've done my best.

The band room explodes with applause. I think I even hear Drew's familiar whistle — higher and louder than any piccolo!

When I look at Bea, her eyes are shiny with tears. "Congratulations," she says. "You deserve the part."

"I haven't won yet," I reply.

She nods. "Yes, you have." She wipes a tear from

her cheek. "You practiced hard. I didn't. I'm sorry I got so jealous when Mr. Ono gave you the part. I should have supported you, not dissed you."

"I'm sorry too," I say. "I didn't start the cookie rumor, but I didn't try to stop it either."

"We both messed up," Bea says.

We're quiet for a moment. "Can we fix things and be best friends again?" I finally ask.

Bea smiles. "*Best* best friends." She shoots up from her chair and gives me a hug.

A minute later, we are standing at the front of the band room with Mr. Ono. Drew and Henry bring him the results from the vote.

"We counted them twice," Henry says, handing Mr. Ono a sheet of paper.

"Thank you, boys," Mr. Ono says, looking at the numbers written on the paper.

Henry wiggles his eyebrows at Bea and me before

returning to his seat. Drew smiles at us, then goes back to the percussion section.

"The winner with thirty-two votes is . . . musician #2!" Mr. Ono says.

Everyone looks at Bea and me. We both reveal the numbers written on our slips of paper.

"Congratulations, Vicka!" Mr. Ono says, shaking my hand. "You will play the piccolo solo at the holiday concert!"

Everyone applauds again. Bea smiles at me. Her real smile. I'd know it anywhere! "Told you so," she says in her teasey way.

Jenny, Grace, and Katie rush up to us after band. "Group hug!" they shout, mauling Bea and me. "You both were great!" Jenny says. "I wish Mrs. Petersen had given the band two piccolos so you could play a duet!"

I look at our huddle of smiling faces. Then I ask, "Where's Annelise?"

Grace snickers. "She was afraid Beatle might make

her eat real bugs, now that she knows who started the rumor."

Bea smirks. "Good," she says. "I think I'll let her stew awhile."

Later that night, Mom makes my favorite meal for supper. Tacos with all the fixings! Plus, pickles. *Sweet* ones!

Sofia sets the table with our fancy dishes. Lucas carefully pours milk into the crystal goblets we only use for special occasions. Dad puts a fluffy couch pillow on my chair. Poco runs in circles, barking and wagging his tail.

"We would have had your favorite meal even if you hadn't won the audition," Mom tells me as we all sit down to eat.

Dad nods. "We're proud of you, Vicka, for practicing so hard! I can't wait to hear you play at the concert!"

Sofia smirks. "I can't wait until it's over. No more piccolo waking me up in the middle of the night."

I make a face at my sister. "But I *like* playing the piccolo. In fact, I'm going to ask Mr. Ono if I can play it all the time!"

Sofia groans.

"Goodie!" Lucas says. "Please pass the pickles!"

Everyone laughs. Poco yips.

"I think this calls for a party," Mom says. She looks at me. "Why not invite your friends to a sleepover Friday night? They can come home with us after we finish decorating the auditorium for the concert."

Sofia sits bolt upright in her chair. "All those giggly girls? For the whole night?"

Mom nods. "*¡Si!*"

"We could practice our ensemble one last time before the concert!" I say, ignoring Sofia's complaints.

"We'll have my famous homemade pizza," Dad puts in. "You could watch a movie — *The Sound of Music* perhaps?"

"A musical sleepover!" I exclaim.

Sofia groans again. "Please pass the *earplugs*."

Lucas jumps up, runs to the hallway closet, and comes back with Sofia's earmuffs. "Here you go!" he says handing them to my sister.

Chapter 10

Drewdolf the Red-Nosed Reindeer

Between practicing our ensemble, decorating the auditorium, and making plans for my sleepover, the next week flies by. I'm still nervous about messing up the solo, but I'm feeling more confident now that things are back to normal between Bea and me. Even with the biggest spotlight in the world pointing at me, I couldn't shine without knowing my BFF is on my side.

Mom and Dad bring me to school on Friday evening to help put the finishing touches on the auditorium before my sleepover tonight and the concert tomorrow. Sofia volunteered to skip decorating and stay home to babysit Lucas. She even said she'd get the pizza stuff ready for my sleepover. Maybe she figures we'll play our instruments quietly if she's nice to us. (We won't!) More likely, it's because my parents gave Joey Thimble permission to come over and help her get everything ready.

Mom and Dad head into the auditorium where some other parents are untangling strings of lights and hanging up giant sparkly snowflakes, turning the stage into a winter wonderland! I go to the band room, looking for the other girls. A bunch of kids are already there, gathered around boxes of props and costumes — reindeer antler headbands, Santa beards, glittery garland halos, and elf hats!

Bea waves me in. I hurry over to where she and Jenny are trying on elf hats with long green tassels. Grace and Katie pull two more hats out of a box and put them on. Annelise takes one from a different box.

Her hat is fancier, with jingle bells on a furry white brim. "Face it, ladies," she says, tossing back her tassel and planting her hands on her hips. "I'm one *bad* elf!"

"You can say that again," Jenny mumbles under her breath. Bea and I giggle.

I put on an elf hat that looks just like Jenny's and Bea's. "We should all wear these for our ensemble," I say, wrapping the long green tassel around my shoulders like a scarf.

"Um, hello?" Annelise says like she's head elf. "The name of our song is 'Green*sleeves*,' not Green*hats*!" She catches a glimpse of her reflection in the mirror that's by the band uniform closet. Turning this way and that, she says, "I *do* look cute in this hat, though. Fine, we can wear them for the concert."

The rest of us roll our eyes in harmony.

Suddenly, Henry wheels Drew into the room on an office chair. Drew is wearing a bright red reindeer nose and a goofy elf hat with antlers! A sprig of fake leaves and berries is sewn to the brim of the hat. It's pulled down over his eyes so he can't see.

Henry gives Drew's chair a spin. "Step right up, folks!" he calls out, like a carnival worker. "It's time for *blind* auditions!" He pats Drew's shoulder. "Let's see if *Drew*dolf the Red-Nosed Reindeer can guess who you are!"

Grace steps forward, giggling.

"Who's there?" Drew says, swinging his head back and forth, the elf hat covering his eyes, the jingle bells jingling.

Grace leans in. "Happy holidays, Drewdolf!" she says. Then she starts giggling hysterically and runs back to us.

"That was too easy," Drew says. "I'd know that giggle anywhere. It was Grace."

"Correct!" Henry says. "Score a point for Drewdolf. Who is next?"

Henry's buddy Tony steps forward. He's built like a bulldog, but he fakes a girlie giggle that sounds just like Grace. "Happy holidays, Drewie!" he says in a high-pitched voice.

Everyone laughs. "Hmm . . ." Drew says, scratching his hat while he thinks. "Is that Grace again?"

Grace squeals. "I don't sound like that!"

"Score a point for Tony," Henry says, giving Drew's chair another spin. When the chair stops, Henry shouts, "Next!"

A few more kids disguise their voices and wish Drew happy holidays. Katie and Jenny fool him. But he guesses Annelise right away. Even her fake voice sounds sassy.

Just then, Dad pops in from the auditorium. "Hey, everyone!" he calls out. "We could use your help setting up the stage. Cookies and punch provided!"

"Are the cookies bug-free?" Henry asks. "I'm insect intolerant." He winks at Bea. "Sorry *Bea*tle, I couldn't resist."

Bea scowls, but then she smiles. "No worries," she quips. "*I* didn't bake them."

Everyone starts heading into the auditorium.

Henry gives Drew's chair another spin. "See ya at the North Pole, Drewdolf!"

"Not if I see you first!" Drew says spinning like a top.

Henry chuckles, then takes off. "Hey, *Bea*tle!" he shouts as Bea, Katie, and Grace follow Annelise into the auditorium. "Wait up!"

Jenny nudges me as Drew's chair spins to a stop. "Here's your chance!" she whispers. "Wish your *crush* happy holidays!"

My eyes go gaga behind my glasses. "How did you know he's my *crush*? Did Bea tell you?"

"No," Jenny says with a sly grin. "You just did!"

She gives me another push toward Drew, then waits by the exit door.

"Is someone there?" Drew asks.

Gingerly, I step up to him. "Um . . ." I say, feeling nervous. Even though Drew can't see me, I still blush as I lean over his shoulder. "Um . . ."

"Hmm," Drew says, thinking. "Is that you, Bea?"

I frown.

¡Ay! My crush thinks I'm my BFF!

"Happy holidays!" I blurt. But I'm flustered because Drew thinks I'm Bea, so I forget to disguise my voice. Plus, I'm nervous so what I actually say is, "*Hoppy* holidays!"

¡Uf!

Drew laughs. "Ribbit!" he replies, butt-hopping in his chair. The jingle bells on his hat ring. I look at the sprig of green leaves and white berries that are also sewn to the brim — it looks exactly like the picture on my "Mistletoe Medley" music.

I gasp, realizing my crush is under the *mistletoe*!

Without giving myself time to chicken out, I lean in close and peck Drew on the cheek!

Unfortunately, Drew hops like a frog just as I kiss him. My nose smashes into his hat. My glasses tilt. The jingle bells ring-a-ling.

Quickly, I step back, straighten my glasses, and

rub my nose. Now I probably look like a red-nosed reindeer too!

"Hey, did you just —?" Drew starts to pull off his hat.

I don't stick around to hear the end of his question.

I take off for the exit, grab Jenny's hand, and yank her out the door!

I don't stop running until we are halfway across the auditorium.

"What's the hurry?" Jenny asks, out of breath. "Did Drew guess who you were?"

I shake my head "I don't think so," I say, glancing back to see if Drew is following us.

"Then what happened?" Jenny asks.

"I . . . I . . ."

"You what?" Jenny persists.

"I . . . I have to find Bea!"

Jenny looks as confused as Lucas does when I try to teach him how to tie his shoes. Even though I'm dying to tell Jenny that I just kissed Drew on the cheek, I have to tell Bea first. We promised to tell each other the moment we first kiss a boy. Best friends always keep their promises!

I look all around the auditorium. Finally, I see Bea by the punch bowl, eating cookies with Henry. I race up to her, grab her arm, and pull her away. When we are safely behind the stage curtain, I stop and look at her.

"Vicka!" she shouts. "You made me spill my punch! Plus, I was in the middle of a very important conversation with Henry! He thinks we should name our band The Beatles, after me." Bea blushes. "This had better be something important."

"It is," I say, breathlessly. "The most important *something!*"

"What is it?" Bea asks, giving me her full attention.

I smile at Bea and spill the biggest secret of my unfortunately average life.

"I just kissed a boy!"

Chapter 11

Starry Wishes

Even though I can barely keep from telling the other girls my secret when we get to my house later, I resist. If Bea were here, I would tell the story to her again, even though I already told it to her three times, and she totally spazzed each time! But Drew's parents invited her out to dinner after we finished decorating. They wanted to thank her for accompanying Drew and Henry's duet. What if Drew still thinks it was Bea who wished him *hoppy holidays*? If he does, then he thinks she kissed him too! Does he even know it *was* a kiss? Or does he think it was just a head clunk? I made

Bea promise to tell me if he says anything about it at dinner.

Joey Thimble is apparently a good cook because he helps Sofia and Lucas make übergood homemade pizza for us. All the girls love it, but I can barely eat five slices because my stomach is in knots wondering what Drew is thinking. And if he and Bea are having a good time together. And if she is starting to crush on him. And if he is crushing on her too!

I, Victoria Torres, need some fresh air! After Dad and Sofia walk Joey home and Mom starts getting Lucas ready for bed, I convince the other girls to throw on coats over our pajamas, switch out slippers for boots, and tromp around in my backyard. The air is crisp and the night sky is clear, so we can see lots of stars. We each pick one and give it a name — Star Annelise, Star Katie, Star Grace, Star Jenny, and Star Victoria.

"Star light, star bright, first star I see tonight," Jenny starts saying the familiar wishing rhyme.

We all join in, looking at our stars. "I wish I may, I wish I might, have the wish I wish tonight!"

Then everyone starts making wishes.

"I wish for ten million dollars to fall from the sky," Annelise says.

She looks around hopefully. But nothing falls. "Fine," she says, pouting. "Make it five million."

"I wish for five million more wishes!" Grace says, giggling.

"I wish I would wake up tomorrow morning with no braces and a movie star smile," Jenny says.

Then Katie steps forward. "Dearest star, I wish Henry would crush on me . . ."

Everyone gawks at Katie. "*Henry?!*" we shriek.

Katie nods. "Yes, Henry. I think he's cute. And misunderstood."

I burst out laughing. "A misunderstood clown," I say. "Plus, I think he might like Bea. But he is kind of cute."

Katie smiles. "What's your wish, Vicka?" she asks.

I look up at Star Victoria. I don't want to make a wish like Katie, even though I secretly wish Drew would crush on me too. But I'm afraid if I told them, the sparkly way it makes me feel would start to fizzle. Plus, Annelise would probably blab it to everyone, including Drew.

"I wish I could play the piccolo perfectly at our concert," I say.

"Boring," Annelise mumbles.

"And I wish Bea were here," I add.

"That's *two* wishes," Annelise says.

"It's my party," I sass. "I get extras."

Just then, the back door opens and Bea steps outside. "What are you guys doing out here? It's freezing!"

"OMG, Vicka!" Jenny exclaims. "Your wish came true!"

"*One* of them, anyway," Annelise snarks.

I lead the pack as we stampede Bea.

"You're here!" I say, amazed that she showed up right after I made my wish.

Bea strikes a sassy pose. "At your service!"

"What was it like, going out to dinner with Drew?" Grace asks, jumping up and down in her clunky boots. "Did he open the door for you? Did he walk you home? Did he kiss you goodnight?"

Everyone squeals like giggly piglets as we pile through the doorway into my warm kitchen.

I tense, waiting for the giggling to die down so Bea can answer Grace's question.

Did he? Kiss her?

But Bea just laughs at all the commotion. "It wasn't like that at all!" she says. "His parents took us to the arcade for pizza. Henry came too. It was a blast! Honestly, I never knew boys could actually be fun. Drew was so sweet. He gave me this."

Bea opens her bag and pulls out a small plastic box. It looks like a take-out container.

"He gave you a doggie bag?" Annelise makes a face. "How *nice*."

"No, it's not a doggie bag," Bea replies. "It's a

corsage! Drew said it was his mom's idea to give it to me as a thank you for playing accompaniment."

Bea opens the box. Inside is a pretty corsage of red and white carnations. "I'm going to wear it at the concert tomorrow night!"

"You're the luckiest girl in the world," Grace says, admiring the corsage. "I wish the cutest boy in our class would give me flowers!"

Everyone starts talking at once, wanting Bea to spill every detail of her time with Drew — if they shared a soda, if they got matching jaw breakers from the candy machine, if they combined their tokens and bought one teddy bear to share. Bea beams with all the attention.

A twinge of jealousy creeps through me. It makes me want to blurt out my big secret about kissing Drew under the mistletoe. I can't help it. I like being the center of attention. Who doesn't?

Instead, I press my lips together, wipe my foggy glasses on my flannel pajamas, and keep quiet. This is

Bea's moment. Sometimes you have to step back and let your friends shine.

"C'mon, everyone," Annelise says, breaking up the crush fest a few minutes later. "It's practically midnight! Let's make popcorn and watch a movie!"

In no time at all, a ginormous bowl of buttered popcorn is sitting on the coffee table in my living room, while we spin around like windmills singing along with the movie's theme song, "The hills are alive, with the sound of music!"

My living room is small, so it's a total mosh pit as we bash into each other, but it's totally fun too. Poco is going bonkers jumping up and down, barking at the top of his tiny lungs! I finally have to put him in the other room before he gives himself a heart attack. If Sofia is sleeping through all this, she must be wearing superpower earmuffs.

Later, we collapse onto our sleeping bags, eating popcorn and discussing important topics, like whether or not Captain Von Trapp is too old to be dreamy, and if you swallow gum, does it stay in your stomach forever, and which of us have started wearing more than just camis under our sweaters.

Mom comes downstairs to check on us. "In all the commotion, I forgot to tell you girls about the socks I bought today at the dollar store." She opens a shopping bag and dumps out six pair of knee socks, all bright green with cute holiday patterns — candy canes, snowflakes, and gingerbread men. "If you like, I could cut them off at the heel, sew up the hem, and you could wear them on your arms for your ensemble performance." She pauses, looking at the *Huh?* expressions on all of our faces. "You know, *green sleeves*?"

Six *Aha!* lightbulbs blink on over our heads. "Greensleeves!"

We dive onto the pile of socks, each grabbing a pair. "Maybe we could decorate them too," I say, pulling a sock on over my hand like a puppet. It comes all the way up past my elbow. "Shiny sequins and funky buttons? Maybe some glitter glue?"

"I'll fix the socks," Mom says. "You set up the craft stuff."

"It's silly for me to wear a pair of socks on my arms," Annelise says as we set out sequins, buttons, and fabric glue on my dining room table. Luckily, Mom has tons of cool supplies. "My dress already has green sleeves. And they *sparkle*."

"But they won't match our sleeves," Jenny tells her impatiently. "Sometimes it's more important to match your friends than to sparkle on your own."

Annelise makes a face at Jenny's comment. But she sits down next to Bea and starts sorting through the button jar, looking for the ones with the most sparkle to sew on her arm socks.

When Bea asks Annelise to please pass the glue, Annelise reaches for the bottle, then hesitates. "FYI," she says to Bea, "I'm sorry about the rumor thing. I'll set the record straight at school. No one will call you *Bea*tle again if they know what's good for them."

Annelise holds the glue out to Bea.

Bea takes it from her. "Thanks," she says. Then she smiles shyly. "But actually, I don't mind the nickname so much. Henry thought of it."

When we finish decorating our arm socks, Grace has a fantabulous idea. "Let's have a dress rehearsal!"

Lucas is already in bed, but Mom and Dad drag Sofia downstairs to help rearrange furniture in the living room while we put together our instruments. I even let Poco out of solitary confinement so he can watch our performance too!

When we finish playing 'Greensleeves,' Mom, Dad, and Sofia applaud. Poco yips and wags his tail.

"Encore!" Dad shouts.

"But that's the only song we know," I tell Dad.

"What about your piccolo solo?" Mom asks. "We'd love to hear it again!"

"Speak for yourself," Sofia grumbles. Dad gives her the elbow.

All the girls settle in while I take out the piccolo. Seeing them there, jumbled together on a heap of pillows and sleeping bags, wearing slippers and fuzzy pajamas, I remember what Jenny said earlier. How sometimes it's more important to match your friends than to sparkle on your own.

Ever since Mr. Ono told us about Mrs. Petersen's gift to the school, I've been eager to shine as the one and only piccolo player in our band. But tonight, I want to be in a spotlight that's big enough to shine on all my friends. For the first time, being in the middle is the only place I want to be.

I tuck the piccolo safely under my arm and dive-bomb for the sleeping bags, smooshing in between Bea and Jenny. The other girls huddle up around us. Then I play my piccolo solo by heart.

Chapter 12

Hoppy Holidays!

At first, I thought I was going to give this holiday card to Drew, but I already gave him a present — right on the cheek! So now I'm writing a message in this card to me.

The holiday concert was fantabulous tonight! The auditorium looked X-tra fab and everyone played X-treemly well!

Our ensemble rocked! We got tons of compliments afterward, both on our playing and on our matching green sleeves.

Drew and Henry's drum and tuba duet stole the show. No joke — they got a standing ovation! After the boys took their bows, they pointed to Bea. She stood next to the piano, wearing her pretty corsage, beaming in the spotlight.

The band performed "Sleigh Ride" better than ever. Mrs. Petersen smiled up at me as I took center stage to play my piccolo solo. I was nervous, but I was mostly honored to make her wish come true! And guess what? I got a standing O too!

I didn't think the night could end more perfectly. But then, after my parents took gobs of pictures of me with Mrs. Petersen and with my friends in our elf hats and fancy outfits, I raced back to the band room to put away my things. Sitting on my piccolo case was a red carnation tied up with a sparkly white bow! A note was attached to it.

Fortunately, the band room was empty because I spazzed! The flower could only be from one person . . . Drew!

I ran to find Bea and Jenny. I showed them the flower and the note. Bea said the XX could stand for "secret admirer" but Jenny said XX could also stand for "kisses!" We were all X-treemly excited!

Tucking the note inside the card, I set it next to the carnation that's sitting in a vase on my nightstand. Then I turn out the lights, hop into bed, and snuggle Poco next to me. He starts snoozing right away.

But I don't fall asleep for a long time. Even with the lights turned out, it's too bright in my room to sleep because I, Victoria Torres, am shining from the inside out!

About the Author

Julie Bowe lives in Mondovi, Wisconsin, where she writes popular books for children including *My Last Best Friend*, which won the Paterson Prize for Books for Young People and was a Barnes & Noble 2010 Summer Reading Program book. In addition to writing for kids, she loves visiting with them at schools, libraries, conferences, and book festivals throughout the year.

Always looking
for her way to shine!

BIRTHDAY
GLAMOUR!

FACE
THE
MUSIC

POMPOM
PROBLEMS

FORMULA
FOR
FRIENDS

Want more Victoria Torres?

Read the first chapter of...

Formula for Friends

As soon as I get home from school on Monday, my little brother, Lucas, races up to me with a puzzle box in his hands. Our grandmother, Abuela, gave him a bunch of jigsaw puzzles recently. Lucas is crazy about putting them together. He's always begging Mom, Dad, Sofia, and me to help him. He asks Poco to help him, too, but Poco just sniffs at the pieces or barks at the pictures of dragons and pirates on the boxes. Poco may look like a tiny Chihuahua, but he's a German Shepherd at heart!

"Vicka, do a puzzle with me!" Lucas begs. He shakes the puzzle box he's holding. It rattles like there's a grumpy snake inside.

"*Please*, do a puzzle with me," I say, correcting Lucas. We're trying to teach him good manners, like saying *please* and *thank you*, and letting other people go first in games, and not sulking or slamming doors when you lose.

"Please, will you do a puzzle with me?" Lucas asks, sweetly. "Pretty please? With gummy bears on top!"

I laugh as I hang up my jacket. Lucas knows I'm gaga for

gummy bears. "Okay," I say. "One puzzle. But then I have to do my homework. The girls and I are chatting later."

By "girls" I mean my friends — Bea, Jenny, Annelise, Grace, and Katie. Bea is my best friend. Jenny is second best. Annelise is sometimes my enemy, but lately she has been a friend. Not my best friend, like Bea and Jenny. Just an *average* friend, along with Grace and Katie.

Usually, we chat later in the week, but another girl in our class, Madelyn, dyed her hair bumble-gum pink over the weekend, so we scheduled an emergency chat. We want to discuss what we think of it and whether or not we would dye our hair a wild color and how long we would get grounded if we did. Once, Bea and I streaked our hair orange with some spray-on hair dye her sister, Jazmin, had. Fortunately, it was the kind that washed out after a few days. *Un*fortunately, I forgot that I had to go to a fancy wedding with my family right after we did it. My parents were not happy that I had orange hair at the ceremony! I got grounded for a week! To make it worse, I still had to go to school. Henry, the class clown, teased me like crazy. Bea too. Sometimes standing out makes you want to hide!

"Yippee!" Lucas cries, hopping up and down like a cartoon bunny. "I love puzzles!" Poco runs in circles around him, barking excitedly. Poco likes it best when everyone in our family is happy.

Mom pokes in from the kitchen. "Oh good, Vicka, you're here. Could you watch Lucas while I run to the store? Sofia isn't home from school yet, and we're out of milk."

Lucas is only five years old, so someone has to watch him.

Usually, my parents put Sofia in charge when they are away, but now that I'm twelve, they let me babysit sometimes.

"Sure," I reply, feeling super grownup. I flick my hair off my shoulders like I've seen Jazmin and her friends do. Sofia is the same age as Jazmin, but her hair is too short to flick. Plus, she doesn't care about acting older. Getting good grades is the only thing that matters to her. "We were going to do a puzzle anyway."

"*¡Gracias!*" Mom says, thanking me. "There's a bowl of grapes in the refrigerator for a snack. Be back in a flash!"

Mom grabs her car keys and heads for the garage.

I turn to Lucas. "I'll get the grapes. You get the puzzle ready."

Lucas and Poco take off for the kitchen. Just as I'm about to follow along, the front door suddenly opens. *Whoosh!*

Sofia storms in.

Slam!

"Mom?!" she shouts past me, like I'm invisible. "Where are you?! I have a *BIG* problem!"

"Mom went to the store," I say, flicking back my hair again. "She put me in charge. What's wrong?"

Sofia looks at me like the answer is obvious. "*EVERYTHING!*" she says, her voice rising like the fur on Poco's back when he's fighting off dragons.

Sofia kicks off her shoes like a ninja.

Thunk!

Thunk!

Ouch!

"Watch where you're kicking, Sofia!" I shout, rubbing my shin.

But Sofia has already stormed down the hall and disappeared

into the kitchen.

¡Uf! Sofia is in one of her unfortunately bad moods. Dad says moodiness is part of being a teenager, along with pimples, braces, and hairy armpits. If that's true, I hope I stay twelve forever!

Suddenly, I remember Mom put me in charge of Lucas. I dash to the kitchen in case Sofia starts throwing forks and knives.

When I get there, Lucas is sitting at the kitchen island, turning over puzzle pieces, so we can put them together. Right now, the pieces are a jumbled up mess. Without looking at the picture on the box, you can't tell how they will fit together or what the picture will look like. But Lucas and I have done this puzzle a zillion times. It never changes. There's always a fire-breathing dragon in the end.

Fortunately, Sofia has calmed down a little. She does not throw the bowl of grapes when she takes it out of the refrigerator. Instead, she slams it down on the counter. *Slam!*

In case you haven't noticed, my sister is an expert slammer.

"When is Mom getting back?" Sophia demands.

"Soon, I hope." I scoot the bowl away from her.

Sofia sighs impatiently. She drums her fingers on the counter, watching while Lucas and I fit pieces of the dragon together.

"Help us with the puzzle," I suggest to my sister. "It will make you feel better."

"I don't want to feel better," she grumbles. "I want to fix my problem!"

"I'm good at fixing things!" Lucas says cheerfully. "Should I get my tool box?"

Sofia rolls her eyes. "A toy hammer will not fix this problem,

Lucas. I have to find someone to join my math club. Now."

"How come?" I ask.

"Because stupid Felicia quit!" Sofia snaps. "Can you *believe* it? Our conference math meet is less than three weeks away!"

Sofia is captain of the Middleton Middle School math club. Every year, the school sends a team to the conference math meet. For the past three years, the Middleton team has lost. This year, the tournament is at our school. Sofia is determined to win the traveling trophy and get her team member's names engraved on a shiny gold plaque. It's all she talks about lately.

"Felicia Armstrong quit?" I ask, surprised. "She's one of the smartest girls in my class."

Sofia makes a face. "Smart?" She grabs a bunch of grapes from the bowl and starts yanking them off the stem like she's plucking the heads off mice. "Felicia is an inconsiderate moron. She accused me of taking the math meet too seriously! She said she was tired of getting bossed around." Sofia chomps a grape. "I'm the team captain. It's my job to tell Felicia what to do! But without her, we don't have a team. We can't compete without six members — two from each grade."

"I'll be on your team, Sofie!" Lucas says brightly. "I'm good at math. Daddy taught me how to count all the way to twenty in Spanish!" Lucas starts counting while he fits the dragon's head in place. "*Uno, dos, tres . . .*"

"Thanks, Lucas," Sofia says with a sigh. "But you're not in middle school. Rachel and Zachary are the seventh graders on my team. Joey and I represent eighth grade —"

Joey is Sofia's boyfriend. He used to be just a goofy kid who lived down the block, but then he grew fuzz on his upper lip and now he hangs out here all the time.

"— and Drew is my other sixth grader."

My hand freezes halfway to the grape bowl. I look at my sister and blink behind my slightly smudged glasses. "Drew is on your team?"

Sofia nods.

I pull my hand away from the grapes. Suddenly, I'm not hungry. Drew is my secret crush. When you like a boy, thinking about him can make you lose your appetite!

". . . *dieciocho, diecinueve, veinte*!" Lucas looks up from the puzzle, smiling proudly. Then he looks at Sofia. "Vicka is in sixth grade, Sofie. She can be on your team!"

Sofia barks a laugh. "I need someone who can work a calculator, Lucas, not just a telephone."

My mouth drops open. "That was *mean*, Sofia! I'm not good enough to be on the math team, but I am good at math. So are my friends."

"Good isn't good enough," Sofia replies. "I need someone who can step up and help us win."

The door to the garage opens. Mom walks in carrying a jug of milk.

"*Finally!*" Sofia exclaims, jumping up and rushing over to Mom.

I jump up too and clamp my arms around Mom's waist. "Take Sofia with you next time," I beg.

"*Pleeeease* take Sofia with you next time," Lucas corrects me.

Mom laughs. "I certainly am popular today! What have I

missed?

Sofia starts gushing about her math club problems. Mom listens while she pours each of us a glass of milk.

"I'm club captain this year," Sofia wails.

"So we've heard," Mom says. She flashes me a grin and hands me a glass of milk.

"It's my responsibility to find a replacement . . . pronto!"

"That means fast, Mommy," Lucas says helpfully. She gives Lucas a squeeze.

I take a sip of milk and hand the last piece of the puzzle to him. Letting the other person go last can also be the polite thing to do.

"I'm *doomed*!" Sofia cries desperately.

"There's an easy solution to your problem, Bella," Mom replies, calmly. Sometimes Mom and Dad call Sofia Bella, which means beautiful and me Bonita which means pretty little one. They're crazy about us.

Sofia's eyes search Mom's face for the answer. "What is it?"

Mom doesn't skip a beat. "Your sister would make an excellent addition to the team. She's good with numbers. She's a quick learner. And she's in sixth grade."

I do a freeze face, gaping at Mom. Is she serious? Me? On the math team? With my bossy big sister? "But . . . but . . . but," I sputter like one of Lucas's toy boats.

"Let me finish," Mom says when Sofia starts firing off her own complaints. "Vicka is family. You live under the same roof. Your bedrooms are ten steps apart. It won't make the work any easier, but it would make it very convenient to study together."

Sofia stops complaining and thinks this through.

"But other kids in my grade are a lot smarter than me," I say, finding my voice again. "Bea, for example. Or Jenny . . ."

"A minute ago you said you were good at math," Sofia cuts in. "And like Mom said, your friends don't live here. You do." She pops a grape into her mouth, chewing on the idea. "I could drill you in math, day and night."

I gulp and look at Mom.

She gives me a confident smile. "I think you're up to the challenge, Victoria Torres. You would be an asset to the team!"

Lucas bounces up and down. "Team Torres!" he shouts, pounding on his finished puzzle.

I look at the fire-breathing dragon.

Then I look at my sister.

"*Pleeease*, Vicka," Sofia begs. "I have to win the tournament!"

I bite my lip, thinking. Joining the math club could be my chance to shine as a smart kid. If we win, I'll get my name engraved on a shiny gold plaque that will hang in the school's trophy case forever! Plus, Drew is on the team. My friends would call me crazy if I passed up a chance to hang out with my crush!

"What do you say, Vicka?" Mom asks. "Will you be on Sofia's team?"

I take a big breath and fiddle with my hair.

"Okay," I say. "Count me in."

Find out more about Victoria's
unfortunately average life, plus
get cool downloads and more at
www.capstonekids.com

(Fortunately, it's all fun!)